Home Fries and Alibis

AN ALL-DAY BREAKFAST CAFÉ MYSTERY

LENA GREGORY

Home Fries and Alibis
Lena Gregory
Copyright © 2025 by Denise Pysarchuk.
Cover design by Dar Albert, Wicked Smart Designs

Beyond the Page Books
are published by
Beyond the Page Publishing
www.beyondthepagepub.com

ISBN: 978-1-966322-27-6

Praise for the Books of Lena Gregory

"Hold on to your plates for this fast-paced mystery that will leave you hungering for more!"

—J. C. Eaton, author of the
Sophie Kimball Mysteries, on *Scone Cold Killer*

"It's fast-paced, [Gregory] never misses a beat. There's mystery mixed with just a small hint of romance and paranormal activity. It's the perfect blend for cozy mystery fans. I'm hoping to read more in this captivating series."

—*Socrates Book Review* on *Occult and Battery*

"The future shows much success for this series! Fun, vibrant characters (as well as a sexy smolder or two for good measure) give the novel just the right tone."

—*RT Book Reviews*

"I loved the protagonist, Cass. She and her friends were very well developed and felt like a group of people I'd like to get to know."

—*The Book's the Thing*

"The book starts off on a fast pace, and is a quick page-turner. Readers will love the charm, wit, and feelings that these characters show."

—*Bibliophile Reviews*

"It has so many great characters and just enough intrigue to keep me on the edge of my seat. The setting was quaint and the author made me want to live there. The mystery is well written and keeps readers guessing till the end."

—*Texas Book-aholic*

"I love a good cozy book right before bed, and this charming story about psychic shop owner Cass Donovan did not disappoint. I stayed up far too late into the evening because I couldn't put it down. A well-crafted mystery with a quirky cast of characters, and plenty of twists and turns to keep you guessing to the end."

—*The Mysterious Ink Spot*

Books by Lena Gregory

Bay Island Psychic Mysteries

Death at First Sight
Occult and Battery
Clairvoyant and Present Danger
Spirited Away
Grave Consequences
A Spirit Seeks Asylum
With a Spirit of Vengeance

All-Day Breakfast Café Mysteries

Scone Cold Killer
Murder Made to Order
A Cold Brew Killing
A Waffle Lot of Murder
Whole Latte Murder
Mistletoe Cake Murder
Battered and Buried
Home Fries and Alibis

Coffee and Cream Café Mysteries

Murder à la Mode
Grounds for Murder
Double Scoop of Murder
Buried on a Sundae
Soft Serve Sleighing
Rocky Road to Murder

Mini Meadows Mysteries

No Small Murder

Cast of Characters

Gia Morelli—Owner, All-Day Breakfast Café
Thor—Gia's Bernese mountain dog
Klondike—Gia's black and white kitten
Savannah Mills—Gia's best friend, former real estate agent, waitress at the All-Day Breakfast Café
Pepper—Savannah's gray and white tabby kitten
Captain Hunter Quinn (Hunt)—Gia's fiancé, Savannah's cousin, captain of the Boggy Creek PD
Leo Dumont—Savannah's fiancé, Hunt's partner
Harley Anderson—homeless man
Earl Dennison—Older man, Gia's first ever customer at the All-Day Breakfast Café
Cole Barrister—Retired, full-time cook at All-Day Breakfast Café
Cybil Devane—Mysterious older woman who often walks in the woods
Alfie Todd—Freelance information analyst
Trevor Barnes—Owner of Storm Scoopers, ice cream parlor on Main Street
Brandy—Trevor's German shepherd
Zeus and Ares—Trevor's guard dogs, Akitas
Willow Broussard—All-Day Breakfast Café's full-time waitress
Skyla Broussard—Willow's mother
Zoe—Owner of the Doggie Daycare Center
Donna Mae Parker—Harley's ex-girlfriend, flower shop owner
Joey Mills—Savannah's youngest brother
Michael Mills—Savannah's brother, works in construction
James, Luke, and Ben Mills—Savannah's other brothers

Chapter One

"What's the point in closing the café and taking a day off if we don't do something fun?" With her elbows propped on Gia Morelli's kitchen table and her chin resting in one hand, Savannah Mills Dumont ran the tip of one long, glitter-tipped, sky-blue nail around the rim of her *Blondes Have More Fun* coffee mug and pouted.

Thor, Gia's Bernese mountain dog, dropped his massive head onto Savannah's lap, rolled his soulful brown eyes toward Gia, and sulked.

"Oh, knock it off. Both of you." Gia stood from where she sat between the two of them and crossed the terra-cotta tile to the counter. If she was going to deal with both her best friend and her traitorous dog moping at the crack of dawn, she was going to need more coffee. She filled her mug then held the pot up toward Savannah, who shook her head moodily. Ugh. She turned and leaned back against the countertop, inhaled deeply the rich aroma of freshly brewed coffee, and took a sip.

It wasn't like she had any specific plans for the day, other than to relax and enjoy twenty-four stress-free hours without punching a time clock, rushing around like there weren't enough hours to fit in everything she had to get done (which there weren't), and fielding complaints from cranky customers. She sighed. In all fairness, most of her customers weren't cranky, just the select few who, despite their chronic complaints, still kept returning to the All-Day Breakfast Café. Perhaps negativity was just a hobby for them. Her gaze flicked back to Savannah and Thor.

Savannah fluttered long, thick lashes that framed big blue eyes Gia had no hope of saying no to. "Okay, fine. What is it the two of you want to do?"

Thor lifted his head and barked once.

Savannah perked right up, straightened in her chair, and offered a sly grin. "Whatever you'd like."

"I'd *like* to go to the nursery for some flowers and plant a garden out front," Gia reminded her.

"Oh, please, sugar." Savannah waved her off with a flick of her hand. "You've been saying that for months, and you and I both know it's not going to happen."

"It might." Especially if Savannah kept insisting it wouldn't. Nothing like a little pessimism for motivation. Besides, she'd heard gardening was a great stress reliever. And, having lived most of her life in New York City, she'd never had the opportunity to give it a try.

"Uh-huh." Lifting one perfectly sculpted brow, Savannah shifted her long blonde hair behind her shoulder, hooked an elbow over her chair back, and pinned Gia with a knowing look. "And what happens the first time you kneel down and find a snake in the weeds? Or a bear lumbers across the yard? Or Rocky Raccoon, apparently your newest pet, stops by for a visit?"

"Okay, that's not fair." It wasn't her fault she hadn't had the heart to get rid of the little varmint after the first time she'd paid a pretty penny to have someone catch him and release him elsewhere. Then, the following day, she'd found him leisurely hanging out on his favorite moss-covered oak branch above her garbage pails, staring at her with an amused look that said, *Ha ha, sucker, I'm not that easy to get rid of.* But the reminder had her second-guessing the idea of a garden . . . again. The chances of her planting and caring for a garden without running into some critter or another were slim to none.

Not that she didn't adore her home in Rolling Pines, she did. The development on the outskirts of the Ocala National Forest in Central Florida was what Savannah had called rural when she'd first found the beautiful little Spanish-style ranch Gia now called home. But it was more like the center of some prehistoric forest—at least, it was to Gia, who'd spent most of her life surrounded by concrete and steel. Of the thousand or so one-acre lots the community boasted, only about half of them had been cleared and built on. That left a lot of swampy forest, home to an abundance of wildlife—bears, coyotes, armadillos, alligators, venomous snakes, huntsman spiders—and that was the end of that. A shiver tore through her. There was nothing Gia feared more than spiders.

Savannah grinned.

"Okay, okay, point made." It was Gia's turn to sulk.

"So . . ." Having won the argument, as usual, Savannah sipped her coffee. "What do you feel like doing? Now that I take it gardening is out?"

Gia pinned her with her harshest glare. "Didn't anyone ever tell you no one likes a smart aleck?"

"Come to think of it . . ." She laughed, the sound musical in the small kitchen. "You may have mentioned it once or twice."

Gia couldn't help but smile. Since there was nothing she wouldn't do for Savannah, who'd been Gia's rock through the most difficult time in her life, it looked like she'd have to suck it up and choose something her friend would enjoy. Which would probably involve an hour's drive to one mall or another followed by the afternoon in a shoe store. Then, of course, they couldn't leave Thor out, so the day would wind up with a hike along one of the many trails Gia had come to enjoy walking—when she didn't come across a body, that is. Or a bear. Or an alligator. Was it too late to change her mind on this? One glance at Savannah and Thor assured her it was.

"All right, we'll—" She was awarded a brief reprieve when the doorbell rang. Although she had no idea who'd be stopping by so early in the morning. She glanced down at her oversized sweats and tattered T-shirt. Oh, well. Nothing she could do about her attire, and answering the door would save her having to make any life-altering decisions. At least, for a few minutes. "I'll just get that."

With Thor on her heels, his long black tail tipped with white wagging furiously at the thought of company, she headed for the front of the house. She peered through the living room window and sighed. She'd have been better off taking her chances with a hike through a viper pit. Of course, not in the new shoes, which would certainly have ridiculously high heels if Savannah was helping her pick them out.

The bell rang a second time.

Then again, a hike through a swamp in stilettos had to beat dealing with Gladys Hoffmeier at six in the morning, or any other time, really. With one last sigh, Gia opened the door to her neighbor from across the street and one house over.

Thor backed quietly away and shifted to stand behind Gia.

Gladys, arms folded across her chest, tapped her foot with about as much patience as Rocky Raccoon on clean-out-the-fridge day. Despite the early hour, the woman was already decked out in a matronly dress, sensible shoes, and full makeup. Her tight red curls clung tenaciously to her head as if they didn't dare droop out of place, despite the humidity. Before Gia could even say good morning or invite her inside, Gladys shifted her hands to her ample hips and glared. "That dog of yours was digging up my yard again."

First of all, it's not your yard. Gia clamped her teeth tightly together to cage the words inside. Since Gladys had come to live with her sister (half sister, Gia reminded herself) six months ago, she'd done nothing but complain and cause trouble in the previously serene community.

Savannah came up beside Gia and lay a hand on Thor's head.

If Gia didn't intervene quickly, the ensuing battle would end up getting out of hand and result in Captain Hunter Quinn, Gia's fiancé, who also happened to be Savannah's cousin, and Detective Leo Dumont, Savannah's husband, being called. Again. It seemed Gladys Hoffmeier had the Boggy Creek Police Department number on speed dial, since they'd banned her from dialing 911 for anything other than a life-threatening emergency the last time they'd been summoned. "Good morning, Mrs. Hoff—"

"*Ms.* Hoffmeier. As I've told you several times now. I divorced my no-good, two-timing ex-husband six months ago, and I refuse to answer to Mrs. ever again." She lifted her chin defiantly.

When Savannah opened her mouth, no doubt to suggest, as she had on several other occasions, that Gladys revert to using her maiden name, Gia reached out and discreetly pinched her arm.

"Ouch." Savannah scrunched up her face, aimed an exaggerated scowl at her, and rubbed the sore spot.

So much for discretion.

"Right. Sorry. Ms. Hoffmeier. As I've told you before, Thor never leaves the house alone. He's either in my fenced yard with me watching him, or he's on a leash." At least, he'd been leashed ever since the first time *Ms.* Hoffmeier had come pounding on Gia's door and accused Thor of knocking over *her* garbage pails. Before that, he'd enjoy romping in the yard while Gia carried in groceries or did outdoor chores. Not that she'd ever let him out of her sight, even then, but at least he enjoyed some freedom.

"And, as I've told you, missy . . ." She lifted a finger, shook it a couple of inches from Gia's nose. "There are no other dogs his size on the block. And the holes on my lawn are too big to have been dug by the Carsons' chihuahua."

"*Ms.* Hoffmeier—"

"I have every bit of damage he's done documented right here."

She tapped the side of her head with one dagger-like, blood-red nail. "As well as a physical copy stashed away. Now, either you get that dog under control, or I will."

Gia seethed, her patience precariously close to tipping over an edge there was no coming back from.

Thor growled low in his throat.

Savannah practically vibrated beside her.

Gia sucked in a deep breath, blew it out slowly, and reminded herself there was a right way and a wrong way to deal with people like Gladys Hoffmeier. She inhaled again. *One, two, three—*

Before she could get any further, Gladys harrumphed. "My half brother-in-law's shotgun hangs right over the mantel, and the very next time—"

"Now, you listen to me, Gladys." Gia's fuse blew. She poked Gladys in the chest, knocking her back a step. "The next time you come to my home and make threats against my dog will be the last time. Do you understand me? I've been patient up until now, but you pushed it too far this time. If you ever threaten Thor again, you'll be sorry you ever moved here."

Her dyed orange brows shot up. "Is that a threat?"

"No, ma'am, that's a promise." With that, Gia took a step back into the foyer.

Gladys pressed a hand against her chest. "Well, I never—"

"Well, maybe you should, honey. It might do wonders for your temperament." Savannah grinned wickedly and slammed the door in her face. "Grr. I'd sure like to cream that woman's corn."

Gia turned and leaned her back against the door, pulled Thor close to her side and weaved her fingers into the thick fur at his neck. Thor was the sweetest dog in the world. How dare that woman threaten to harm him.

"Can you please call . . ." But when she lifted her gaze from Thor, Savannah already had her cell phone pressed against her ear.

She held up a finger and spoke into the receiver. "Yes. Thank you."

"Leo?" Gia asked the instant she disconnected.

"Nope. He's too easy-going," she snorted. "This time, I called in the big guns."

Uh-oh. On second thought . . . Never mind. Gladys Hoffmeier deserved whatever she got. "Is Hunt coming?"

"Of course he is." She hesitated, caught her lower lip between her teeth, and glanced up at Gia. "You do realize she's probably going to claim you assaulted her and try to press charges, right?"

Gia swallowed hard, more concerned about what might happen to Thor if she was arrested and forced to leave him alone at the house. He'd be safer at the doggie daycare center than he would be home. "If Hunt does have to take me down to the station, will you call Zoe and see if she'll take him?"

"Don't you worry about a thing. I'll make sure Thor is taken care of. I'll either take him with me, or if I have to go with you, I'll call Zoe."

Gia nodded. Tremors tore through her. Still angry from the confrontation, or a diminishing adrenaline rush? She had no idea. But she did know one thing: she'd do whatever it took to keep Thor safe.

Seeming to sense trouble, Klondike, Gia's black and white cat, weaved between her and Thor's feet and purred. The chunk missing from the tiny cat's ear served as a reminder that Thor had saved her and her two siblings' lives. She scooped Klondike into her arms, then knelt and hugged Thor tight. "Don't you worry, Thor. That woman won't hurt you, and I won't let her come back here and frighten you again."

He snuggled close, resting his big head on her shoulder, and whimpered.

Savannah gave her a couple of minutes before hooking her elbow and helping her to her feet. She patted Gia's arm. "There, there, sweetie. If I know Hunt, which I do, he'll be here faster than a barefoot jackrabbit on a hot greasy griddle in the middle of August."

Laughter blurted out. "You're quoting SpongeBob to me now?"

"Hey, whatever it takes." She waggled her brows. "Now, come on, don't let that woman stay in your head one minute longer."

"You're right." Gia set Klondike down. She shifted the curtains aside and peered out the front window.

Benjamin Stettler knelt on his front lawn across the street fiddling with something, but there was no sign of Gladys anywhere.

She let the curtain fall shut and turned to go make more coffee. If her morning so far was any indication of how the rest of her day off would play out, she was going to need it. Maybe she'd just start opening the café on Mondays too. It seemed a day off was more trouble that it was worth.

Savannah scrolled through her phone contacts as she walked, her pale blue silk robe fluttering gracefully around her legs, then settled on one and pressed the number. "Hey, Alfie. You busy today?"

Gia couldn't make out his response, just a muffled voice coming over the line as Alfie Todd—friend, computer expert, and all-around good guy—answered.

"Yup. It involves tech, and it's super important," Savannah said, then hung up the phone and grinned. Mischief danced in her eyes. "Alfie's on his way."

"Okay, spill, so what's the plan?" Because, based on the look in Savannah's eyes, there most definitely was one. And whatever it was, hopefully, it would fix Gladys Hoffmeier. Savannah might be a kitty cat most of the time, but when someone messed with those she loved, she turned into the fiercest tiger.

She shrugged. "We're going to see to it Gladys Hoffmeier can't make any more accusations against you or Thor. That woman has issued her last threat."

Chapter Two

"So, basically, what you're telling me is, there's nothing you can do?" Gia leaned a hip against the kitchen counter, folded her arms, and lifted a brow at Captain Hunter Quinn. This day just kept getting better and better. Even his dark good looks, eyes like melted chocolate, and good-ole-boy charm couldn't do anything to improve her mood. She rubbed her hands up and down her arms to ward off a chill, despite the oversized peach sweatshirt she'd put on over her T-shirt and white shorts.

At least, Hunt had the good grace to wince. "I'm sorry, Gia. I can go over and talk to Mrs. Hoffmeier. Again. But I can't arrest her."

"And why not?" Savannah propped both hands on her hips and jutted her chin, fast losing patience with his logical attitude and ready to go to battle—whether with Gladys or Hunt, Gia wasn't sure mattered. Sweat beaded her temples, despite the powder-blue tank top she wore with her cutoff jean shorts. "She threatened to shoot Thor."

"Come on, Savannah." He held up a hand to halt her protests. "Technically, she only threatened to harm Thor if he came onto her property. I can't arrest her for that. She hasn't actually committed a crime."

"Yet," Gia grunted and lowered a hand onto Thor's head. The thought of anything happening to him had her on the edge of an all-out panic attack. She thought she'd overcome the attacks that had plagued her throughout her husband's trial, their divorce, and then his murder investigation. Perhaps she was wrong. Suddenly too hot in the cozy kitchen, she whipped the sweatshirt over her head and tossed it onto the back of a chair.

The big dog seemed to understand they were talking about him, and he leaned his side against Gia's leg.

"So . . . What . . . ?" Savannah crowded against Thor's other side, a line of unity Hunt dare not cross if he knew what was good for him. "You're saying we have to wait until she actually does something to him before you'll take action?"

"That's not fair, Savannah, and you know it." Hunt hooked his thumbs in his jeans' pockets and frowned down at Thor. The hunter green T-shirt he wore darkened his eyes, or perhaps that was anger or frustration. Either way . . .

And Gia had a moment of sympathy for him. Hunt loved Thor just as much as she and Savannah did. But the law was the law. And Hunt couldn't change it. Not even for his fiancé or his favorite cousin.

Leo stood beside Hunt, his gaze lowered to the floor, no doubt torn between obeying his captain's decision and earning his wife's wrath. The poor guy had no hope of winning there. He was either doing double duty if he defied Hunt or sleeping on the couch if he crossed Savannah. A fact he seemed to understand, since he smoothed a hand over his crew cut a few times, tugged at his T-shirt collar, and shot Hunt a pained expression.

A chill descended again in Gia's usually homey kitchen, and the warm rustic cabinets, natural stone countertops, and Mexican tile backsplash could do nothing to ward it off. Nor could the sunshine pouring through the window above the sink and spilling over the terra-cotta floor tile. She didn't bother reaching for her sweatshirt again. What would be the point? This chill had nothing to do with the actual temperature in the room or the cozy surroundings. And the only thing that could chase it away would be to get rid of Gladys Hoffmeier. Which it didn't seem Hunt would be able to do. At least, not yet.

"So, now what?" Gia's gaze bounced between Hunt and Leo, searching for answers neither seemed to have.

"There isn't much you can do except watch Thor when he goes out . . ." Hunt held up his hands to ward off her protests before she even had a chance to voice them. "Which I already know you do. And make sure you drop him off at daycare when you go into the café. If you have to go anywhere today, take him with you. If you can't, call me and I'll pick him up and keep him with me at the station."

It was the best he could offer under the circumstances, but knowing that didn't help her feel any better.

"On the bright side," Hunt offered, "we haven't yet received a call from Mrs. Hoffmeier, so maybe she decided not to press charges against you."

Gia snorted. Not very ladylike, but an honest reflection of how she felt. "And if she does call, are you going to arrest me?"

Although there was no mistaking the note of challenge in her voice, Hunt chose not to engage. "We'll deal with that if it happens. For now, let's not borrow trouble."

"Sure." She stared down at Thor. From the day she'd picked him up from the shelter, he'd been her whole world. No way would she let Gladys or anyone else do anything to harm him. No matter what.

"Gia?" Hunt leaned over and looked up into her eyes, his voice stern. "I mean it. No trouble. You two stay away from Mrs. Hoffmeier. Hopefully, this will all blow over."

"Yeah, sure, whatever." She waved him off. The desire to weave her fingers into his thick, wavy, dark hair gripped her, but only to give it a good yank and bring him to his senses.

He pinned Gia with a hard stare. "Gia . . ."

There was always a chance Gladys's sister would get tired of her and toss her out. Hmm. That might be an idea. She'd spoken with Miley before, only to say hello or how's the weather the way neighbors do, but the woman seemed nice enough. Maybe she could talk to her about her sister, get her to reason with Gladys. "I said okay. But I don't have to like it."

Instead of arguing further, Hunt simply pulled her into his arms.

She stiffened at first, her anger taking a moment to subside, but then she settled against him. If only she could stay there all day, cocooned in his protective embrace. Then she remembered she was too busy being annoyed with him and sighed. "Do you two want coffee?"

Hunt dropped a kiss on the top of her head before stepping away, apparently satisfied their discussion was ended and she'd accepted his proclamation.

Clearly, he didn't know her as well as he should considering they were engaged to be married.

He narrowed his eyes at her.

Then again . . . Maybe he knew her better than she thought.

"Thanks, anyway, but we've got to get going."

Giving up on getting help from the police, Gia hooked his elbow and walked him toward the front door. Best to get him and Leo out of there so she and Savannah could come up with a plan. Because no way was she letting this go. "Are you going to be around for dinner?"

He stopped in the foyer, turned to face her, and tucked a strand of curly dark brown hair that had come free of her sloppy knot behind her ear. "I'll tell you what, why don't I stop and pick up Xavier's after work, and we'll all sit down together and enjoy a meal?"

Memories flooded her. It seemed so long ago, the first time Hunt had arrived on her doorstep with Xavier's Barbecue. He hadn't known her well then, and he'd been smack in the middle of her ex-husband's murder investigation, in which she'd been the prime suspect and he the lead detective, and yet he'd shown up with Xavier's, shocked Savannah hadn't introduced her to it sooner. He'd had no reason to trust her back then, and yet he had, even when not many others in town had felt the same. But Hunt had ignored the conspicuous stares and the whispered suspicions. He'd welcomed her, made her feel at home, helped her. It might have started because she was Savannah's best friend, but he'd gone past that, because despite what he saw every day in his chosen career, he believed there was good in people. And he'd believed in her.

She opened her mouth to speak, got choked up, and settled for simply nodding.

"Hey." Hunt tugged the strands of hair that had managed to spring loose again, playfully this time. "Don't worry about anything, Gia. We'll get this all straightened out. I'm not going to go over and give that woman the opportunity to insist I arrest you, but I will increase patrols in the area, especially at night. But, as long as you keep Thor close, I'm sure everything will be all right."

"Thanks, Hunt. I know you'll do whatever you can." *And Savannah and I, with Alfie's help, will do what you can't.* She figured it wise to keep that tidbit to herself. But it reminded her, she needed to get him and Leo out of there before Alfie showed up and they got suspicious. "And Xavier's sounds great. I'm looking forward to it."

"Me too. I'll see you around eight." His smile sent her heart all aflutter.

"Perfect." That should give them enough time to work out whatever plan played mischievously behind the innocence in Savannah's big blue eyes. Because there was no way she'd be saying goodbye to Hunt and Leo, or letting them off that easily, if she didn't have something else in mind. "I'll see you then."

Hunt leaned in and kissed her, not the quick peck she'd expected but a long, lingering promise of more. When he shifted away, his gaze remained on hers, his brown eyes melting toward dark chocolate. "I'll see you later."

She resisted the urge to twine her fingers into the dark hair curling over his collar. "Sure."

With one quick, cocky grin, he swung the door open and then stopped short.

Alfie Todd had just lifted his hand to knock, and he jerked back. The black duffle bag slung over his shoulder, which probably weighed more than he did, swung back, threatening to topple him over. "Uh . . ."

Hunt lifted a brow at him, then turned his gaze on Gia. "Gia . . ."

"What?" She aimed for innocence, but the high-pitched squeak probably damaged her credibility.

Thankfully, Savannah stepped between them, hooked Alfie's elbow through hers, and offered a brilliant smile. "Come on in, Alfie. It's good to see you. Alfie's just going to give Gia's security the once-over. You know, make sure everything's updated and all that pesky nonsense. We'll see you guys at dinner."

"Dinner?" Alfie rubbed his flat belly.

"Xavier's Barbecue, from what I overheard," Savannah said smoothly. "Want to stay?"

"You bet." He nodded eagerly. "I'd never pass up Xavier's."

As he spoke, Savannah guided him inside and practically threw Hunt and Leo out. She started to close the door behind them.

Hunt splayed a hand flat against the door and poked his head back inside. "All I'm going to say is, Gladys Hoffmeier had better not show up at the station later with doorbell footage of any of the three of you anywhere near her house. Are we clear?"

Gia lifted her chin defiantly.

Savannah swung her long blonde hair over her shoulder and gave an indignant snort.

Alfie's gaze bounced back and forth between them. He drew his brows together. "Huh?"

"Gia . . ." Hunt warned.

"Yes, dear."

He shook his head as she closed the door behind him.

"So." Alfie petted Thor's head, then rubbed his hands together in anticipation. "Can I assume your summons has something to do with that nasty woman who moved in with Miley Davis?"

"You bet it does." Savannah headed toward the kitchen, her heels clicking against the tile. "That woman threatened Thor."

Alfie's brown eyes went wide. His mouth firmed into a thin line. "Are you kidding me?"

"Nope."

"Okay, so what are we going to do?"

Warmth spread through Gia. It hadn't been too long ago that she'd been alone, frightened, and in trouble. Now, as soon as trouble came calling, she had a whole list of people standing beside her, sometimes even in front of her. Tears pricked the backs of her eyes, and she quickly looked away. Needing a moment to regain her composure, she busied herself pouring fresh coffee and setting the mugs on the table.

Alfie set his bag on a chair, slid the zipper open, and hooked the handles of a plastic bag from inside. He set it on the table, dug in, and took a seat. "I figured you guys hadn't had breakfast yet this early, so I stopped for bagels."

"Thanks, Alfie." Though just the thought of food had a lead lump settling in her stomach. Or maybe that was dread. Either way, she opened the fridge and pulled out butter, jelly, and cream cheese then set them on the table along with plates and knives.

Savannah grabbed a pitcher of fresh-squeezed orange juice and three glasses.

Even though she didn't feel like eating, Gia plucked a still-warm cinnamon raisin bagel out of the bag and inhaled deeply, the warm, spicy scent reminding her of fall in New York. And, as happened more and more lately, the reminder didn't bring a pang of regret or homesickness, only memories better left in the past. She buttered the bagel, cut it into four pieces, and set it on her plate. Maybe the bread would help absorb some of the acid burning in her gut.

Savannah popped an everything bagel into the toaster over, then leaned back against the counter and folded her arms across her chest. "Okay, so, how do you want to handle this?"

Gia shrugged and filled all three glasses with orange juice before setting the pitcher aside and dropping onto a chair. "I thought you had a plan in mind?"

"I do." She smiled, all sweet and innocent. "I want Alfie to install security cameras all around your property."

Alfie paused mid-chew, then ratcheted into overdrive, chewing frantically then practically choking down his bite of bagel. He was already nodding vigorously as he chased the lump with a swig of juice. "I could do that. I can even make sure some of them point toward Mrs. Hoffmeier's yard. That way, we might catch whatever is digging up her yard and getting into her garbage and exonerate Thor."

"I had a thought about that too." Savannah shot Gia an apologetic smile as she sat with her toasted bagel. "You know, even if the woman is meaner than a wet panther, it is possible she actually believes it's Thor. Bernese mountain dogs have become very popular, and I've seen more than one in the development, though usually with an owner or on a leash. I suppose it's possible one of them is getting out, and Gladys thinks it's Thor."

"Huh." Gia hadn't thought of that, but Savannah was right. And if Gladys had gone about her complaints differently, Gia might have considered that and mentioned it. She bit into her bagel, the taste of cinnamon bursting on her tongue, then took her time ordering her thoughts.

If it was another dog, and Gladys had seen him, she could possibly have mistaken him for Thor. On the other hand, if she hadn't seen him, it could be any animal damaging her half sister's property. Either way, the cameras should give them some idea what was going on. "Is it legal to point the cameras at Miley's house?"

Alfie shrugged. "I don't see why not. As long as they're on your property."

"All right, then. Let's do it." Not that they hadn't discussed installing cameras before; they had. It was just one of those things she'd never gotten around to. But now that Thor could be impacted, it was time to make it a priority. Besides, aside from keeping an eye on the comings and goings at Miley's, it would be interesting to see what went on in her own yard at night as well. Ever since moving to Rolling Pines, she'd witnessed all kinds of critters, including a couple of bear cubs playing beneath a tree in her yard and an overzealous raccoon. She could only imagine what went on that she didn't see. "Can you install them today?"

"You betcha. I just have to run out to pick up cameras."

"Well, then . . ." She glanced at Savannah, who started buttering her bagel. "I guess we know what we're doing today. Sorry it wasn't something more interesting or fun."

"Don't worry about it." She waved off the apology with the butter knife still clutched in her hand. "Thor's safety is way more important. Besides, next Monday you can make it up to me with a spa day."

"You've got it." Even if it wasn't Gia's favorite way to spend a day, it helped Savannah relax, so she was all in. As long as the situation with Gladys Hoffmeier was resolved by then.

"Great." Alfie hesitated. "But, um . . ."

Just what she needed, another problem. "What?"

"Well." He winced and peered at her from the corners of his eyes. "It's just that Hunt gave me an idea."

"What kind of idea?" Though she was reluctant to hear his answer. Alfie tended to get a bit overenthusiastic.

"When he mentioned Gladys showing up with doorbell footage." He hesitated.

"Okay."

"I mean, it wouldn't be legal, technically. *If* we got caught." He tugged at his polo shirt collar. "But I could possibly hack Miley Davis's doorbell camera footage. If she has a subscription that includes the ability to access video footage, I might be able to see exactly what already went on over there without having to wait for your cameras to pick up something new."

Gia sucked in a deep breath and blew it out slowly. She normally drew the line when it came to doing anything illegal. Or, at least, she had since getting engaged to Hunt. How would it look for him if he had to arrest his own fiancé? Not exactly a great career boost. Then again, it would certainly show how honest he was. Of course, she wouldn't want to put him in the position of having to make a choice like that. And she definitely wouldn't want to get Alfie in any trouble.

Thor whined once, propped his head in Gia's lap, and rolled his eyes up at her.

"Let's get the cameras installed." She stared into Thor's big brown eyes, so filled with trust and unconditional love, lay a hand atop his head, and her resolve strengthened. "Then we'll hack the doorbell footage and see if we can prove Thor is not her culprit."

Chapter Three

Gia held her breath and extended her arms while Alfie balanced precariously atop a ladder and reached under the eaves to adjust one of the new cameras he'd spent all day installing. Of course, if he toppled off, she had no hope of catching him. If anything, she might just cushion his fall when he landed on her.

"Gia?" A male voice she didn't immediately recognize startled her, and she jumped and bumped into the ladder.

It swayed for a brief moment before Alfie managed to regain his balance and steady the ladder. He shot her a scowl.

She winced, "Sorry, Alfie," then turned to the newcomer. "Hey, Ben. What's going on?"

"Sorry about that." Ben Stettler, her neighbor from across the street, gestured toward Alfie then tilted his cap back to scratch his head, still staring up at him. "I couldn't help but notice you've been installing cameras. I don't suppose that has anything to do with your run-in with Gladys Hoffmeier this morning?"

"Actually . . ." She let the thought trail off, unsure how much information she should share with Ben. If word got around that she'd installed cameras facing Gladys's yard, the woman might cause even more trouble for her, might even rethink her decision not to press assault charges against Gia. Then again, when Hunt had called earlier to let her know he'd heard from Gladys regarding the incident, he'd been fairly confident he'd talked her out of doing so. Still . . .

Ben gestured vaguely behind him. "I was fixing my sprinklers when I saw her storm over here with an eyeful of venom and figured nothing good could come of it."

The anger Gia had worked so hard all day to curb came rushing back. "She accused Thor of digging up her yard and getting into her garbage, even though I've told her a million times Thor never leaves the house without me."

"I can attest to that. I've never seen the big guy running off by himself. Unlike others in the neighborhood."

Hope surged. "Other Bernese mountain dogs?"

He stroked his graying stubbled chin thoughtfully. "Not that I've noticed, but there is a black Lab that likes to roam. Maybe she mistook one for the other?"

Gia shrugged. Not that it wasn't possible, but the two dogs had completely different builds. "I'm not sure she's ever even seen a dog in the neighborhood. I think she's just making an assumption because her yard was dug up and her garbage gone through. The pest is more likely to be a bear or a raccoon than a dog anyway."

"Probably. Or even a coyote. It's not like we don't have plenty of those." He hesitated, seemed to weigh what he was about to say carefully, then apparently decided to trust her, or at least test the waters for a reaction. "You're not the only one in the neighborhood she's giving a hard time, you know."

"Oh?" Unfortunately, with running the café, she didn't have much time left over to gossip around the development. The thought suddenly occurred to her that she didn't know many of her neighbors all that well. Sure, she recognized some of them from the café, and others to wave at when she pulled in and out of her driveway or walked over to Savannah's—a rare occurrence considering the abundance of critters that still terrified her. "I didn't realize she was harassing anyone else. I thought I was her only target."

"Not by a long shot." He winked, and his warm blue eyes sparkled with humor. "Although, you may be her favorite."

"Gee, thanks." But she laughed, some of the tension beginning to dissipate.

"Even Irene Kellerman, the head of the HOA, has butted horns with good ole Gladys." He paused, glanced around for a few seconds then leaned in closer. "From what I hear, Irene refers to her as the grumbling old windbag."

"Not very flattering."

"Nope." He shrugged. "But it says a lot."

"I suppose it does, but I'm still surprised. I've only met Irene a few times when I stopped in to pay my HOA fees, but she seems super sweet." She'd always been kind to Gia, had welcomed her warmly when she'd moved in. At least, before the rumors had started flying. "What did Gladys give her a hard time about?"

"Irene hasn't said, but . . ." He waggled his bushy gray eyebrows. "Inquiring minds definitely want to know."

Gia grinned. Truth be told, she was curious as well.

"And just the other day, I saw Carter Marx . . ." He hooked a thumb over his shoulder. "The guy that lives all the way up at the far end of the development?"

Gia shook her head. "I haven't heard of him."

"His property is the last in Rolling Pines. It butts up against the forest. The other day, he was walking his pit bull down here, and I saw him give her a scathing look when he walked past and she was outside getting her mail. Let's just say, if looks could kill, that woman would have keeled over on the spot."

A small flare of hope flickered but died just as quickly. No way could anyone mistake a pit bull for a Bernese mountain dog. Still . . . it was interesting to hear. Maybe the woman just hated dogs, or dog owners. "You live right next door to her; have you had any problems? Or seen anything unusual?"

"Nah. Just the same old, same old."

And his pair of snow-white Pomeranians could never be mistaken for Gia's hundred-plus-pound black, rust, and white dog. "And you haven't had any run-ins with her?"

He stiffened for an instant then relaxed, his eyes darting toward Alfie, who'd just started down the ladder. Then he spared a quick glance toward Gladys's house before returning his attention to Gia. "I mind my business, and I expect her to do the same."

But that wasn't really an answer, was it? And now Gia's curiosity was piqued even further.

Alfie hopped off the last rung and rubbed his hands together. "There. All set."

"Well . . ." Ben lifted his baseball cap, smoothed back long salt-and-pepper hair tied in a ponytail at his nape, and hitched his overalls up over his beer belly by the straps. "I'd best be going. I just wanted to stop by and let you know if you need a witness, you know, with that shoving thing and all, I'll be happy to say I saw Gladys come onto your property and start in with you."

"Thank you, Ben. I really appreciate that." Though it didn't sound much like minding his own business to Gia. But what did she know? Maybe Savannah would have an idea what had gone on between him and Gladys. Because Gia was sure something had.

"You bet, dear. Just being neighborly. Have yourselves a good day now." He tipped his cap and headed down the front lawn, then crossed the narrow road without bothering to look both ways.

Alfie frowned after him. "What was that all about?"

"No idea." But she had bigger things to worry about. "Are the cameras all set up?"

"Yup." He tilted his head up toward the sky, where dark clouds billowed and threatened to unleash their fury. "Just in time too, from the looks of the sky."

"No kidding." A jagged bolt of lightning raced to the ground not too far in the distance, and one fat raindrop splattered against the window. "We should probably get that ladder down."

"I'll grab it in a minute. All that remains is teaching you how to use the cameras." He held out a hand and wiggled his fingers in a come-ahead gesture. "Give me your phone."

Gia pulled it out of her shorts pocket and handed it over.

"Why don't you go ahead in and see what Savannah's up to? I'm just going to set up your phone to access the footage remotely, double-check that we have clear shots of Gladys's property, and adjust the cameras if necessary before I clean up out here."

"Sure thing. You want something to drink?"

"Yes, please. The colder and sweeter the better."

"You've got it. Savannah made sweet tea last night." Her mouth watered at the thought. "I'll have it ready when you come in."

"Thanks," he tossed over his shoulder as he bent and started collecting tools and dropping them into his bag.

Gia left him to it, knowing he liked everything just so and would prefer to handle it himself. She pushed open the front door, wiped her feet on the mat, and shut the door behind her.

Thor raced from the kitchen, skidded on the hardwood floor as he started across the living room, and nearly took her out when he reached the foyer.

She couldn't help but laugh as she ruffled his fur. "Yes, Thor. I missed you too."

Savannah grinned from behind him. Apparently, she wasn't even comfortable leaving him unsupervised in the house. "You would think you'd been gone for a year the way he pounces when you walk through the door."

"I know, right." Gia laughed. "I can't imagine anything more wonderful."

Savannah simply offered a smug smirk and turned to go finish whatever she'd been up to in the kitchen before Gia had come back in. There was no need to say I told you so—again—since she'd been the one to insist Gia needed a dog after moving to Rolling Pines. Still, it was one of the best decisions Gia had ever made. "Come on, boy. Let's get you some dinner."

At the mention of food, Thor barked once, turned, and trotted toward the kitchen.

Once all the chaos had quieted, and at the mention of food, Klondike emerged from beneath the couch and offered a nonchalant meow before sticking her tail in the air and sauntering after Thor as if she had all the time in the world.

By the time Gia finished feeding them both, walking Thor, and washing her hands, Savannah already had the table set for dinner, and Alfie had returned.

He took her place at the kitchen sink, looking out over the yard, and held Gia's phone up so she and Savannah could view the screen over his shoulders. "So, first, you open the app."

"What do you mean open it?" Gia asked innocently.

"You click it with your finger." He spared her a glance that said *you've got to be kidding me*, and she grinned. "Very funny. Even you can't be that technologically challenged."

"Hey." She punched his arm. "Watch it, buddy."

He shrugged. "Not my fault you don't know a computer chip from a potato chip."

"Of course I do. You can't dip a computer chip."

"Ha ha."

Despite the less-than-ideal circumstances, it felt good to relax with friends, and Gia found she was looking forward to dinner. Determined not to ask Hunt or Leo anything about Gladys Hoffmeier until after they'd enjoyed their meal, Gia returned her attention to Alfie's tutorial. While she'd been out back with Thor, she'd decided she was excited to see what kind of wildlife might make an appearance on the videos. Of course, once she had, she might be too afraid to ever walk outside again. But she'd cross that bridge when she came to it. Just the other day, she'd managed to get the garbage to the curb despite the black snake (which she could thankfully identify as non-venomous) curled in a sunny spot a few yards away. A chill raced through her, and she shivered.

Thankfully, there was a knock on the door before her thoughts could run too rampant.

"I'll get it." Without waiting for a response, she headed for the door.

Thor beat her there and whirled to face her, his tail, along with the rest of him, wagging wildly.

"Okay, Mr. Impatient. I'm coming." She reached to open the door then hesitated with her hand hovering over the doorknob. She should have looked out the window first. "Who is it?"

"It's me, Hunt. Open up."

She could practically hear the grin in his voice, and she whipped the door open, then waited for Thor to give him an excited hello to avoid being battered or knocked over in his exuberance.

"Hey, there, buddy." Hunt laughed as he returned the greeting with his one free hand and an equal amount of enthusiasm.

Once Thor's excitement turned to Leo, Gia stepped into Hunt's arm for a hug. The tantalizing scent of barbeque wafted from one of several bags cradled in his other arm and hooked over his wrist. As much as she'd have loved to remain in his embrace for a moment longer, her stomach growled, reminding her she hadn't eaten anything since the half a bagel she'd managed to choke down for breakfast. Plus, there was no sense lingering in the doorway any longer than necessary. Not that Thor had ever run out, but now was definitely not the time to risk it.

She stepped back, ushered Hunt and Leo inside, and shut the door behind them.

"Hey, don't I get a turn?" Savannah squeezed between Thor and Leo to kiss her husband hello.

Gia crossed the living room with Thor trotting happily, tongue lolling, at Hunt's side and Klondike purring as she weaved between his feet, no doubt hoping for a sampling of the delicious aromas coming from the bags he carried. "Forget it, you two. You both already ate."

"Yeah, right." Hunt lifted a brow at her, knowing full well she'd share with both of them.

Since he wasn't wrong, she ignored the insinuation. "So, how was your day?"

He sighed. "Long."

When they reached the kitchen, Hunt said hello to Alfie then set the bags on the table.

While Gia started emptying containers from the bags, he retrieved a chair from the desk in the living room and set it in front of the fifth table setting.

Alfie sat and rubbed his hands together, then unfolded a napkin and tucked it into his shirt collar. "Man, I haven't had Xavier's in a long time. Thanks."

"You bet." Hunt washed his hands, grabbed a soda from the fridge, and sat down next to him then stared pointedly. "So . . . did you get Gia's security all squared away?"

He swallowed hard and shifted his eyes. "Uh-huh. Yup. Yes siree."

Hunt narrowed his gaze on Alfie.

To his credit, Alfie returned his stare with a minimal amount of squirming. "Whatever goes on outside tonight will be captured on video. If nothing else, we'll be able to prove Thor never left the house since I pointed cameras at all of the exits, windows as well as doors."

"Hmm." Seemingly satisfied, Hunt ripped open a foil bag and started piling barbeque chicken onto his plate.

Leo and Savannah sat beside each other, and Gia dropped onto the seat next to Hunt. Idle chitchat filled the room as the food was passed around and doled out, lightening the tension that had weighed on her all day.

Gia forked in a bit of smashed potatoes and barely resisted groaning out loud when the rich flavors of butter and fresh garlic burst on her tongue. "I can't believe I almost forgot how good these are."

"We really need to do this more often," Savannah said and bit into a buttered biscuit.

Gia had to agree.

"Could you please pass the coleslaw." Alfie gestured toward the tub in the center of the table. When Hunt handed it to him, Alfie swallowed and wiped his mouth. He added a few spoonsful to his already loaded plate. "So, Hunt, did Gia tell you Ben Stettler stopped by?"

"No. What'd he have to say?" He wiped barbeque sauce from his fingers then grabbed another napkin.

Xavier's was nothing if not messy. "Apparently, I'm not the only neighbor Gladys has been complaining about."

"You're not even the only neighbor she's called the station about." Since Leo was scooping potato salad onto his plate like it was going out of style as he spoke, he missed the glare Hunt aimed at him.

But Gia didn't, and she lowered her fork, lifted a brow at Hunt, and clasped her hands on the table in front of her. "Oh no?"

He sighed and wiped his mouth with a napkin, took a long swig of his Pepsi, then cleared his throat—no doubt running through how much he'd have to share in his mind, along with what he could get away with keeping to himself. Hunt tended to guard his information more closely than Leo, even among friends. "Apparently, Ms. Hoffmeier has a nasty habit of arguing with her neighbors, then calling the station and demanding we come out. Then, when we send a patrol officer, she conveniently forgets what had her so riled up or just says she resolved things with the neighbor."

"Huh." Gia frowned, running the scenario through her head but unable to come up with any reason she'd continue to call the police then change her mind about needing their services. Unless . . . "Do you think someone was threatening to hurt her if she didn't recant her statements?"

Hunt shrugged. "According to all of the officers who've responded, every one of whom I spoke with today, she didn't seem to be under any duress. She usually just waves them off and sends them on their way. That's why we had to finally issue a warning—if she called 911 again for anything other than a dire emergency, we were going to cite her."

"And did she stop?"

"Mostly. Though she just switched to calling the non-emergency number instead." Apparently finished talking, he picked up spareribs.

Thor lifted his head, barked once, then scrambled to his feet and bolted for the front of the house.

"What in the world . . . ?" Gia stood, lifted her napkin from her lap and tossed it onto the table, then went after him. "What's wrong, boy?"

He stood at the front door, barking and growling low in his throat.

"Gia, step back." Hunt hooked Thor's leash to his collar then opened the front door. "Close the door behind me and wait here."

She started to do as he said, but Alfie grabbed her arm. "Hold up, Hunt."

He paused, gaze darting around the yard as Thor continued to bark.

"Here." Alfie handed him his cell phone then clicked the screen to start a playback of the security footage the camera had recorded.

Hunt kept one eye on the video while scanning the yard with the other.

Gia, Savannah, and Leo crowded around Hunt to watch the screen, where a very large black bear lumbered across the front yard, paused to paw at something for a moment, then continued on his way and disappeared behind a row of bushes in the direction Thor was yanking on the leash, straight toward Gladys Hoffmeier's house.

"Well, well, well." Alfie took the phone back from him and grinned. "Looks like we might have found our culprit. Mystery solved."

While Gia sure hoped he was right, she had a nagging suspicion this might not be the last she'd hear from Gladys Hoffmeier.

Chapter Four

Gia yawned and poured her second cup of coffee, then dropped onto a stool at the All-Day Breakfast Café's front counter. She spun the stool around to look over the dining room and soak in the cozy feeling of home she and Savannah had created, exactly as Gia had imagined before she'd come to Florida. Visions of the life she'd hoped for had gotten her through the toughest of times, and even so, the reality of her new life far exceeded any hopes she'd ever imagined.

The distressed bamboo flooring and paintings of local scenery were the perfect backdrop for round tables of varying sizes, covered in navy blue cloths, that dotted the room, and the light-colored wood chairs with homemade cushions that surrounded them. Homemade centerpieces and candles adorned every table, lending to the homey atmosphere.

She closed her eyes for a moment and inhaled deeply. With everything in the kitchen prepped for the breakfast rush and the dining room clean and restocked, she took a moment to savor the rich aroma of coffee and the fresh muffins she'd just finished loading onto glass-domed platters. She was just debating blueberry or banana chocolate chip when a soft knock at the front door brought her up short.

Earl Dennison, the elderly gentleman who'd been her first ever customer and had since become a dear friend, yanked the red fisherman's cap from his thick gray hair and waved at her through the window.

She smiled back at him and hurried to unlock the front door, then held it open as he paused to hug her and then walked inside. "Good morning, Earl. You just saved me from a lonely breakfast of carbs and sugar."

"Happy to oblige, my dear. Instead, now you can eat with me." He grinned. "And indulge in carbs and fat. A much better choice, if I do say."

She simply shook her head. Earl once said his late wife, Heddie, hadn't approved of his breakfast choices so he'd taken to eating breakfast out, and it had become a lifelong habit he'd continued even after she'd passed away. Not that Gia could blame Heddie for trying to get him to eat healthier. Bacon, sausage, three scrambled eggs, grits, two biscuits with gravy, and now the addition of Gia's home fries wasn't exactly the healthiest way to start the day. Although, for a rail-thin man in his eighties, Earl was far from fragile.

She debated leaving the front door unlocked, but she still had an hour before opening, and she wanted to spend some time enjoying the quiet and the sense of nostalgia that had gripped her this morning. Besides, Savannah and Cole each had their own keys, so it wasn't like she'd have to get up again to open the door when they arrived. And, this morning, she needed as much downtime as she could get before jumping into the fray.

"Rough night?" Earl frowned at her as he hung his cap on the coatrack and headed for his usual stool at the end of the counter.

"Thor had me up all night." Pacing, barking, whimpering. She still had no idea what had him so spooked, but her guess was the confrontation with Gladys and the stress Gia had been under afterward. Thor had always been very in tune to her moods.

"Is he okay?"

Gia rounded the counter and poured a mug of black coffee, then set it in front of him as he sat. "He's fine, he just—"

A knock at the front door made her pause before she could return to her own seat, and she glanced over to find Alfie frantically waving both arms over his head. She muttered, "What in the . . ." as she headed for the door.

Then, he turned toward something behind him and stepped away from the door.

Savannah, her attention on Alfie, stuck her key in the lock and pulled the door open, then allowed him to precede her.

"What's wrong? Did something happen?" Scenarios rocketed through Gia's head, all of them tragic. Then she paused, took a breath, and reined in her self-inflicted terror. Thor was safely tucked away at the Doggie Daycare down the street, and Zoe would have contacted her immediately if anything had happened to him. "Is Hunt okay?"

"Yeah, yeah, yeah, everyone's fine." Alfie frowned and scratched his head. "Or, at least . . . Actually, I'm not sure."

"What are you talking about?" Gia hooked one of his arms, Savannah the other, and they guided him to a stool. "Sit, Alfie, calm down. I'll get you coffee."

"No." He shot from the stool and fumbled his phone toward her. "No coffee. Just look at this, and tell me what you see."

Her gaze lingered another moment on Alfie, trying to determine if he was actually okay.

Sweat beaded his brow, trickled down his temples, and caught up in the brown hair he'd recently buzzed for the summer. He swiped an arm absently across his forehead then pointed at the phone. "Just hit Play. Please. It's urgent."

As if she couldn't tell by his bizarre behavior. Not that Alfie didn't tend to be . . . excitable. He did. But this was way over the top, even for him.

Savannah set her purse on the counter and dropped her key ring inside, then took the phone from Gia and set it on the counter. Sparing one long glance at Alfie, she hit Play.

Gia held Alfie's hand, willing him to take a beat, as she bent over the phone beside Savannah.

Earl rested a hand on the counter on Savannah's far side and tilted his head to watch the video.

Alfie craned his neck to see past Gia. "I still have the whole video, but I've cut to the important part. Just watch at about one minute in."

Gia leaned closer. Given that the image was of Gladys Hoffmeier's garage, she figured she was watching footage from the camera Alfie had placed at the corner of Gia's house. Her gaze ran along the front lawn, but she didn't see anything out of the ordinary, just some night bugs swirling around in front of the camera, most likely drawn by the floodlight that sat beside it. She tipped her head and followed the line of the garage toward the back. From this angle, she had a good view of the side of the garage, the small door that sat toward the back, the window . . .

"Wait." She squinted, leaned even closer. A dark shadow separated from a row of hedges Ben Stettler had planted not long after Gladys had moved in with Miley. Only for an instant, then it once again merged with the rest of the shadows. "What was that?"

Alfie wiped his head and flopped back onto the stool. His complexion paled. "Just keep watching."

As Gia stared at the shadows, she must have missed Gladys emerging from the front door, but she rounded the front of the garage, stopped to glance over at Gia's, then continued up the side of the garage toward the back of the house. Then, the shadow emerged once again. A large man? A bear? Gia couldn't be sure. But Gladys lurched back, and then the shadow enveloped her, and she was gone.

"Wait. What just happened?" Savannah hit Pause, backed the video up, and replayed it.

A split second. Two tops. And Gladys was just gone. Disappeared into thin air. "When did you find this, Alfie?"

He glanced at his smartwatch. "Five minutes ago. Maybe less. I was up all night working, had a freelance job due today, and I had to put in the time to get it done. I loaded up with caffeine and pulled an all-nighter."

Which wasn't all that unusual for him. Working as a freelance information analyst, he could set his own schedule and often worked through the night to allow himself freedom during the day. What was unusual was the agitated state he was in. "Alfie."

"Right. Right. So, uh, I didn't find it until a few minutes ago, but the time stamp on the video puts the . . . um . . . incident? at around two this morning."

"Around two?" Gia frowned as she thought back, tried to remember each time Thor had gotten restless and she'd stared at the clock moving too quickly toward the time she'd have to get up for work. "That's one of the times Thor started barking."

Alfie shoved a hand over his buzz cut, as if not quite used to the lack of hair. When his gaze shot to Gia, his eyes were as wide as breakfast platters. "Do you think she was abducted?"

"Who'd want her?" Savannah waved it off. "And even if someone did abduct her, I have no doubt they'll return her right quick."

Gia scowled at her.

"What?" She shrugged and pouted. "Just sayin'."

"Maybe aliens?" Alfie rattled on. "Or Skunk Ape? Some people claim to have seen him out in the woods behind Rolling Pines, you know."

Gia massaged her temples. Somehow, she doubted Florida's version of Big Foot had abducted Gladys Hoffmeier. Still . . . Rolling Pines did butt up against a vast amount of forest, thick forest, where anything, or anyone, could be hiding. A chill raced through her, and she shivered and wrapped her arms around herself.

"All right." Earl, ever the voice of reason, cleared his throat. "Let's all calm down and look at this rationally. What does the video really show? A shadow and Gladys. It could have just been a gust of wind blew one of the hedges toward the house just at the exact moment Gladys rounded the back corner, making it appear as if she just"—he snapped his fingers—"vanished into thin air."

"Like an optical illusion," Savannah agreed. "Hmm."

Earl fished a pair of reading glasses out of his shirt pocket and put them on. "Can you run it in slow motion, Alfie?"

He was already shaking his head.

"How about a live shot of what's going on right now?" Earl suggested.

Hands shaking, Alfie tapped the screen a few times, and a live shot of the house came into view.

Gia scanned the side of the garage, the hedges, lingered for a moment on the spot the shadow had emerged from, then continued studying the live footage. It seemed all was quiet enough. A lizard darted from behind the air-conditioning unit, startling her, and she jumped and pressed a hand against her chest.

This was ridiculous. She was starting to feel like some kind of spy. Surely, Gladys was entitled to some semblance of privacy in her own—

Her gaze caught as it passed the front door, skipped back. "The front door is standing wide open."

"What the . . ." Savannah looked into Gia's eyes, any sense of playfulness gone. "Gia—"

"I'm already on it." She yanked her cell phone from the pocket of her capris and hit Hunt's number. "Come on, come on, answer . . ."

"Hey, Gia. Everything all right? Don't even tell me Gladys Hoffmeier already started—"

"Hunt, listen, I am calling about Gladys, but it's not what you think. I know this is going to sound strange, all things considered, but Alfie just came into the café with footage from during the night. And it's . . . well . . . weird." The words tumbled over one another as she tried to spit them all out as quickly as possible, the surety that Gladys needed help a burning niggle in her gut. "It shows Gladys walking out of her house around two this morning, going around the side of the garage, and . . . Okay, I know this isn't going to make sense, but it looks like a shadow comes out from the hedges, and then she's just . . . gone."

"Hold up. What do you mean, gone?"

"She just vanishes with the shadow." She paused, waited for him to say something—anything—to offer some rational explanation for what made no sense. When he didn't, she continued. "Then, he pulled up the live footage, and it looks like her front door is standing open."

"Now?"

"Yes."

"And there's no sign of her?"

"No. Nothing." Gia's heart raced, and sweat slicked her hand clutching the phone in an iron grip.

"Okay. Uh . . . give me a couple of minutes. I'll get someone to do a welfare check, but could you ask Alfie to text me the footage?"

She relayed the message.

"Sure," Alfie answered as he fumbled with his phone. "You bet. I'm doing it right now."

"He's sending it now, Hunt. Do you think something happened to her?" Because as angry as she was with the woman, she didn't want to see any harm come to her. "Oh, and I don't know if this has any bearing, but Thor had me up all night, barking, growling, pacing. He wasn't himself. Maybe someone was over there and he sensed it?"

"I don't know yet, but I'll get back to you as soon as I hear anything."

"All right. Thanks, Hunt."

"Hey." Hunt hesitated. "You okay?"

Was she? Probably. Just anxious if the lead weight in her gut was any indication. And guilty. She could have gotten up during the night, checked the video on her phone. If she had, would she have called Hunt? Woken him in the middle of the night to go in search of a shadow? Maybe. She just couldn't be sure. All she did know was that she could have gotten up, checked the video, looked out the window, taken Thor out to see what was going on. And if it was a bear or some other wild animal? Either way, instead of getting up and doing something, she'd simply put her pillow over her head and tried to get some sleep. "Yeah, just nervous. Let me know as soon as you find her, okay?"

"Sure thing." And with that he was gone.

With nothing left to do, she stuffed the phone back into her pocket and dropped onto a stool. "He's going to have someone do a welfare check."

"Leo's on his way back up there. He'd only left for work a few minutes ago, so he's turning around to go back up." Savannah dropped her phone back into her purse and turned to Gia, tears shimmering in her big blue eyes. "You guys know I was only kidding about any kidnappers returning her, right?"

"Hey, of course we do." After Savannah's abduction from a house she'd been showing when she'd worked as a real estate agent, she'd been extremely sensitive and prone to crying episodes. Since retiring from real estate and going to work as a waitress for Gia, it seemed she had begun to heal. But this, it seemed, might have hit too close to home.

Her chin trembled and she looked down to her clasped hands. "Do you think something happened to her?"

Earl hooked an arm around her shoulders and led her to a stool. "There, there, dear. I'm sure everything will be fine."

Alfie sat beside her and patted her hand.

"I'm sure she's okay." Gia got up, rounded the counter, and poured coffee. Then she set a mug in front of Savannah, filled one for Alfie and one for Earl, and shoved her own guilt aside for later. "But even if she's not, we did everything we could. As soon as we realized something was wrong, we called for a welfare check. Even after she treated us the way she did."

"I'd never have wished anything bad on her." A tremor tore through Savannah. "Especially not that."

Gia leaned forward on the counter, clutched both of Savannah's ice-cold hands in hers, and pressed her forehead against Savannah's. "Of course, we know that. Everyone knows how sweet you are and that you wouldn't wish anything bad happening to anyone, not even your worst enemy."

"All right. Okay." She nodded, sniffed.

Gia handed her a tissue. "I'm sure it'll all be fine."

But, by the time her cell phone rang a few minutes later, and Hunt's name popped up on the screen, the dread that had settled in her stomach had turned to outright fear.

Chapter Five

Gia pulled into her driveway, parked, then simply sat and watched the crime scene unfold in her rearview mirror. She and Savannah had left immediately after the call from Hunt confirming their worst fears.

"I can't believe she's really dead." Savannah made no move to get out of the car or turn around to watch the beehive of activity surrounding Miley Davis's house, where Leo had found Gladys Hoffmeier dead in the backyard, feet from where the shadow engulfed her. "I feel awful."

"Savannah . . ." Gia took her hand, wrapped both of hers around it and willed it to warm. "You couldn't have known. And, it's not like Gladys hadn't done anything to deserve your anger, she had. Several times."

"Yeah, but still . . ." She looked down, shook her head.

"She wasn't a nice woman, Savannah. Being dead doesn't change that." But Gia was dealing with her own share of guilt, as well. How many times had she wished Gladys would just go away? But not like this. She'd just wanted her to move out, or even just leave her alone.

"I suppose." She continued to sulk, unable to embrace any sort of comfort. "I just wish there was something we could have done."

Gia wouldn't be deterred. They may not have been able to help Gladys when she'd been attacked, but they could maybe help her now. If only she could get Savannah to see and accept that. "The only thing we can do for her now is cooperate with the police so they can nab her killer and see that she gets justice."

Savannah sucked in a deep breath and blew it out slowly. She lifted their joined hands, squeezed, then released Gia and reached for the door handle. "You're right. Come on. Let's get this done with."

"Sure thing." Determined to do what she could to help the investigation, Gia climbed out of the car. A quick glance at the branch stretching over her garbage pail assured her Rocky Raccoon wasn't lounging above waiting to pounce. Not unexpected, since he usually made himself scarce when there were people around. Still, she slammed the door quickly behind her. No sense taking any chances he might look for a place to hide and take refuge in her car—again.

Leaving the keys and her bag in the car, she started across the street. She hadn't yet decided whether to go back to work, but she'd have to pick Thor up at daycare either way. For now, the café was in good hands with Cole Barrister in front of the grill and Willow and Skyla Broussard running the dining room. "Did Leo tell you what happened to her?"

Savannah shook her head. "No. Did Hunt say?"

"No, just that she'd been killed."

"Do you think it could have been an accident? Or maybe a heart attack?" Savannah sounded so hopeful.

Gia couldn't blame her. The thought that a killer might have been standing right across the street from her house while she'd slept soundly, or rather tossed and turned all night, had a dull ache throbbing at her temples.

Crime scene techs hurried in and out Miley's front door, investigators rounded the garage and headed toward the backyard, and crime scene tape stretched the full width of the property. Lookie-loos had begun to gather, and it seemed about half of Rolling Pines' residents were standing in the street or on Gia's and Ben Stettler's front lawns. The other half were currently causing a traffic jam entering the development that Gia was glad to have made it through. "I'm pretty sure it wasn't an accident or a medical emergency."

"One can hope," Savannah argued.

"Yeah." Though she didn't hold out much.

Hunt emerged from the house, studying something on a tablet, his expression hard. When he lifted his gaze for a moment and spotted Gia, he handed the tablet off to a tech and crooked his fingers at her in a come-ahead gesture.

Gia glanced at Savannah, met her gaze filled with dread and held it for a moment, then took a deep breath and started across the street with Savannah glued to her side. When they reached the crime scene tape, Hunt lifted it so they could duck under. "Thanks for coming. I really appreciate it."

"Sure. No problem." Gia swung a hand to encompass the entire chaotic area. "I take it Gladys didn't die of natural causes?"

"No. I'm sorry to say, she did not."

"Do you have any suspects?" Gia eyed the crowd. Could Gladys's killer be among them, studying his handiwork even as the investigation unfolded? The thought turned her stomach.

He lifted a brow at her but didn't bother answering until after he pulled a notepad and pen from his shirt pocket. "Probably everyone she ticked off over the past however long. How long ago did she move in with Miley? Do you remember?"

"You mean exactly? Or around?"

"As precise as you can be."

Gia shrugged, but she tried to think back. It was tougher than she'd have expected, considering Florida's weather didn't change all that much, making timing anything by seasons difficult. But she did remember seeing the moving truck when she'd been setting out her reindeer decorations for Christmas. "I'd say about six months."

"And that jibes with what she said the other day, about having divorced her husband six months ago," Savannah added. "I'm pretty sure that's when she moved in with her sister."

"Half sister," Gia reminded automatically.

"Right. Speaking of . . ." Savannah frowned and looked around. "Where is Miley?"

"We don't know yet." Hunt jotted something on the pad, flipped back a few pages, and skimmed whatever he had written there.

"Do you think something happened to her too?" Savannah's chin trembled, and she caught her lower lip between her teeth as she scanned the scene, her eyes darting from the techs to the yard where Gladys had disappeared.

Hunt glanced at Gia and drew his brows together.

She gave him a quick, discreet head shake. No, Savannah did not seem to be dealing with this well. She'd been so traumatized after her attack, but she'd been steadily improving. Gia worried Gladys's murder would be a setback she didn't need. But now wasn't the time to discuss her fears with Hunt. She'd just stick close to Savannah for the remainder of the day until Leo could get home. At least, by then, some of the shock would have worn off, and they could get a more accurate read on her emotional state.

"We have no reason to believe any harm came to Miley, Savannah," Hunt assured her.

She nodded, inhaled deeply, and let out a slow shaky breath. "Okay."

Seeming to decide she was going to keep it together, Hunt turned to Gia. "I already saw the video Alfie sent, but can you expand on it at all, Gia? Did you see anything, hear anything, notice anything unusual?"

She was already shaking her head before he could finish. She'd already gone over and over it so many times in her mind, she could pull the entire night up at will. "Thor acted restless all night, pacing, barking, growling. Unusual for him, but I figured it was all the stress from yesterday. First, Gladys came over all in a huff."

Hunt scratched his head and narrowed one eye.

She paused, swallowed hard. "I don't mean—"

"Hey. It's okay, Gia. I know you weren't particularly fond of the woman, but when you thought something might have happened to her, you called me right away to help. There's no changing who she was or how she treated people. All we can do now is try to find out what happened to her and bring her killer to justice."

"You're sure she was umm . . . ?" She checked Savannah in her peripheral vision.

Hunt must have caught the gesture because he answered without her having to finish the question. "I'm sorry, but yes, she was definitely murdered."

It was on the tip of Gia's tongue to ask how, but she refrained. The last thing she or Savannah needed was a blow-by-blow account. Right now, all that mattered was giving Hunt whatever information he needed to catch Gladys's killer and then tending to Savannah.

Hunt seemed to breathe a sigh of relief when she didn't push the issue.

"Anyway, after that fiasco, Alfie was here all day installing the cameras, Ben Stettler stopped by to chat, Savannah and I were both stressed and tense all day, which I know Thor picks up on." She thought back through the night, noted each instance Thor jumped up and started barking, berated herself for not getting up and looking out the window.

"Hey." Hunt pocketed his notepad, reached for Gia, and tilted her chin up so she'd have to meet his unflinching stare. "This is not your fault. None of it is."

"If I'd have just gotten up and looked out the window, I might have seen something." She drew in a deep shuddering breath and lost her battle against the tears. "I might have been able to save her."

Hunt wrapped his arms around her, drew her close until there was nothing left of the world but the two of them. He spoke quietly next to her ear, barely loud enough for her to make out the words. "You couldn't have saved her, Gia. She was beaten, badly. It wouldn't have taken more than a few minutes. You saw on the video how quickly she was grabbed and pulled behind the garage. Even if you had looked out the window or at the video, you couldn't have done anything in time to save her. Her body might have been found sooner, but that's all."

She swallowed hard, willing the bile to burn its way back down her throat. "Where was she?"

He gestured vaguely in the direction of the backyard. "Beneath a tarp that appears to have been covering an old bike."

Gia nodded against his chest, confident he'd hold her in his embrace as long as she needed him, and also knowing he needed to get back to work. And Savannah needed her. If not for that, she might not have been able to peel herself away from the comfort he offered. She swiped the tears from her cheeks. "All right. I'm okay. Thank you for that. Is it okay if I take Savannah home now?"

"I don't want to go home." Savannah averted her gaze.

"We can't stay here . . ."

"I know. I . . ." She struggled for control. "I know we can't stay here, but I don't want to be at your house right across the street or at my house still in the development. Can we please just go back to work?"

"Of course. Sure." Gia pulled her close and glanced at Hunt. "If you need anything else, I'll be at the café. Do you want me to leave you my phone so you can access the other cameras?"

"Thanks, but that won't be necessary. Alfie already sent me the login information." He kissed Savannah's cheek. "Don't worry, cous. I promise we'll find who did this. And, if it makes you feel any better, it seems to me whoever did it knew her and targeted her specifically. I don't think you have anything to fear, and if I did, you know I'd be insisting you guys stay in the apartment over the café for the time being."

"Which we can do if it makes you feel better," Gia offered.

Savannah nodded, sniffed, and offered a shaky smile. "Thank you. Both of you. But I'm fine. Really. It's not bringing back the past or anything. I just feel bad about the unkind thoughts I had toward her and kind of emotional and—uh . . ." Her eyes went wide, and she stared off into space. She pressed a hand against her stomach and turned a sickly shade of green.

"Savannah? You okay?"

"What?" She shook off whatever random thought had gripped her, and the queasiness seemed to pass. "Oh, right. Sorry. Anyway, I'm fine, but could we please go back to the café?"

"Sure. You'll let us know if you hear anything, Hunt?"

"Of course."

"Thanks." She turned away from him and started across the yard with Savannah tucked close.

Even more of a crowd had gathered in the few minutes it had taken to speak to Hunt. Gia didn't recognize many of the onlookers, and she couldn't help but wonder if these people were all her neighbors or if word of the murder had spread and drawn a crowd from outside the development. She recognized Irene Kellerman, head of the Rolling Pines Homeowners Association, who stood transfixed, apart from the bulk of the crowd. A few strands had come free of her usually perfect blonde updo, and she toyed with the pearl stud in her ear. When she spotted Gia looking at her, she shied away.

Gia started toward her. Ben had mentioned Irene having had words with Gladys over something. Maybe she—

A man she'd never seen before caught her attention. Disheveled dark hair hung in greasy strands down his back. He wore torn jeans, but not fashionably so, and his oversized, drab olive-green sweatshirt on a day that was topping ninety before lunch made him stand out from the crowd. But it was his behavior that had drawn her attention. He was fidgety, rocking back and forth, sparing furtive glances toward the police officers. When his gaze met hers, he whirled and took off deeper into the development.

She pulled out her phone, called Hunt, and explained what had happened. With no hesitation, he went after the guy. She'd leave that to him, but in the meantime, she'd already planned to speak to Irene, and what better time than the present? But when she returned her attention to the spot the woman had been standing in, she was gone. Gia spent a couple of minutes searching the crowd for her, but to no avail. She'd have to catch up with her later.

"Come on, Savannah, let's get back to the café." Because Savannah's well-being was more important to her than anything else.

Chapter Six

When they reached the café, there was plenty of street parking, so Gia pulled alongside the curb. "You hungry? I could ask Cole to make us some breakfast before we start working. Willow and Skyla are already here, so we don't have to get to it right away."

"Um, yeah, I could eat. But I just realized I need to run out for something first." She grabbed her purse and slung it over her shoulder, then hopped out before Gia could say anything more.

Gia stuck one foot out and stood then called after her. "Hey, Savannah, wait. What do you need? I'll take a ride with you."

She turned, smiled, and waved. "That's okay, but thanks. I'll only be a couple of minutes. Why don't you get Cole to fix us something, though. I just suddenly realized how hungry I am."

"All right, what do . . ."

But Savannah had already turned and hurried down the sidewalk toward her blue Mustang convertible.

"Hey, there, beautiful."

Gia jumped, startled, and whirled toward the man's voice that had come from directly behind her. She pressed a hand against her chest to keep her heart from jumping out. "Oh, for crying out loud, Trevor, don't sneak up on me like that. What are you trying to do, give me a heart attack?"

Trevor Barnes, who owned Storm Scoopers, the ice cream parlor down the road from the All-Day Breakfast Café, simply shot her his adorable grin. "Sorry about that."

"Uh-huh." But she wasn't so sure. He looked more contriving than contrite.

He shook the brown hair that hung a bit long in the front out of brilliant blue eyes. "So, listen, I just dropped Brandy off at daycare, and Zoe told me what was going on out by your house. I can't even believe it. That's awful."

"I know, right. And it seems to have Savannah completely on edge." She looked in the direction Savannah had gone, as if suddenly her behavior would make sense. It didn't.

"Well, you can't really blame her," Trevor offered.

"No, especially after all she's been through." Gia grabbed her bag from the car, closed the door and clicked the lock button, then dropped the keys into her bag. Together, she and Trevor lingered on the sidewalk outside the café. Sunshine beat down on her, cocooning her in warmth.

Main Street bustled around them, for a weekday morning in Boggy Creek anyway. People hustled in and out of the quaint, old-fashioned shops and along the cobblestone sidewalks. Kids, out of school for the summer, rode bikes and scooters while their parents kept a wary eye on them as they chitchatted among themselves. Not surprising, considering there'd been a murder in Boggy Creek and no suspect had yet been found. While Rolling Pines usually didn't attract much attention, Gladys's death would put it dead center on the gossip map. "I just hope Hunt finds the killer quickly—"

"Wait! What?" Trevor tripped over his own feet, regained his footing, then held up a hand and shook his hair back out of his eyes again. "What are you saying about a killer? Zoe said some woman was harassing you, accusing Thor of tearing up her yard and pulling out her garbage. What are you talking about?"

Huh. Perhaps the Boggy Creek Rumor Mill was on the fritz today. Although, Rolling Pines sat on the outskirts of town, so maybe things were just moving a little more slowly than usual. Either way, she wondered if word had yet reached the café. If it hadn't already, it would soon enough, considering the growing crowd in town. "Come on in and I'll catch you up over coffee."

"Sure." He glanced down the street in the direction Savannah had gone, then entered through the door Gia held open.

The instant she stepped inside and spotted the Bailey sisters, decked out in their Sunday best, all hope of a peaceful span of time before the gossip ratcheted up tanked. The two elderly sisters, Estelle and Esmeralda, were Boggy Creek's very own Woodward and Bernstein. They had ears everywhere, and they missed nothing. Gia was pretty sure they sometimes knew things before they even happened. If they were sitting front and center in the café dining room, rumors had already spread. And if they hadn't, they would soon enough.

Gia smiled and zipped past them with a nod and a cursory good morning. Since they only had coffee in front of them, she'd have time to get back to them after she updated Trevor and the others.

Earl still sat at his usual spot along the counter, no doubt hanging around for an update, and so that he could pitch in if they got busy and needed a hand.

Alfie sat at a small corner table hunched over a laptop. She had no clue what he was doing, but the fact that he was doing it at the café so he'd be there in case they needed him warmed her heart.

A few scattered customers dawdled over breakfast or coffee, maybe just enjoying the company, maybe waiting for news of the latest murder. Either way, the dining room would be okay for a little while without her attention.

"Trevor, why don't you gather everyone at the big table in the back, and I'll update you all at once." No sense going over and over the events of yesterday and this morning with each person individually. "I'll see if Cole can get away from the grill for a few minutes."

"Sure."

Leaving him to do that, Gia walked into her office and dropped her bag onto the visitors' chair in front of her desk. She sighed and glanced in the mirror, then took a moment to smooth her usually curly dark hair, which had turned to frizz in the Florida humidity, back into a bun. She used a wipe to clean the smudged makeup from beneath her eyes, then considered herself as put together as she was going to get under the circumstances. She grabbed her apron from a hook on the back of the door, tied it on, then crossed the short hallway to the café kitchen.

Cole, who'd started out as a part-time cook after he'd decided retirement didn't suit him and had since become a full-time employee, hummed a Beach Boys tune as he used a long spatula to flip three eggs at once without breaking a single yolk. As Gia crossed to him, he scooped up the eggs and lay them on a plate atop a mountain of corned beef hash.

"How are things going, Cole?"

He shot her a quick smile without missing a beat. "Can't complain. How about you?"

When the toaster popped up two slices of rye bread, Gia checked the ticket, buttered them, and set them on a small plate Cole had already set out. "I don't know if Earl caught you up, but we had a situation out at Rolling Pines last night."

"He did." He turned to her then, looked into her eyes. "I'm sorry. And I'm sorry for what went on with Thor. I hope he's okay."

Gia couldn't help but smile. "Thanks, Cole. Thor's good. He trotted off to daycare happy as could be this morning."

"Glad to hear it." He scanned the next ticket, opened the fridge and grabbed a stainless-steel bin filled with vegetables, then scooped some onto the grill. While they sizzled, he scrambled eggs with milk, salt, and pepper, then poured them out onto the grill.

"When you finish that ticket, I thought we'd do breakfast for everyone and meet at the back table to eat." She checked the clock over the cutout between the dining room and kitchen as she set the completed order down for Willow to pick up. It was just about one. Things should be relatively quiet for the next little while.

"Sure thing. You want me to just throw together a platter?"

"That sounds great."

"How many?"

She counted in her head. Assuming Savannah returned soon, it would be her and Gia, Trevor, Alfie, Earl, Cole, Willow, and Skyla. "Eight."

"Got it." He folded the veggies neatly into the eggs, then added a few slices of cheese to the top and plated the omelet.

She set the plate onto the cutout. The scent of hash, eggs, and vegetables teased her, making her stomach growl. She'd been just about to have breakfast when Alfie had come in and she'd never gotten to eat.

In companionable silence, she and Cole worked together to fill several platters with bacon, ham, sausage, scrambled eggs with cheddar and red pepper flakes, and pancakes. Gia added bowls of grits and home fries. "Oh, Cole, I've been meaning to tell you. I tried a new recipe for the dinner menu."

"Oh? How'd it come out?"

"I think it's pretty good. I meant to bring some in this morning, but I was in a rush to get Thor to daycare early enough that I could talk to Zoe, and I forgot."

"No problem. Cybil and I can stop by later if you want. Or you could bring it in tomorrow morning."

Gia thought about it. While having good friends over would certainly be nice, she had no idea what was going on at the crime scene across the street or what kind of crowd might still be up there, or even if she could go back home or needed to stay at the apartment upstairs. "How about we do it over the weekend?"

"Sounds like a plan." He buttered several slices of toast, bagels, and English muffins and piled them on a plate. "Are you going to tell me what it is or keep me in suspense?"

She grinned. Cole was so much more than a cook. He'd become her right hand at the café as well as a close friend and had single-handedly increased her dinner rush a thousandfold. "Short rib hash, but instead of regular potatoes, I used sweet potatoes, then topped it with fried eggs and avocado slices."

"Mmm. That does sound good. Can't wait to try it." He hefted the biggest platter, and instead of setting it on the cutout, he carried it out to the dining room himself.

Gia set the smaller plates on the cutout so Willow and Skyla could start setting them out. She enjoyed having Cole test her recipes. He had a good sense of what worked, especially for the dinner menu, when she wanted the food to be a little more filling without sitting too heavily. Her dinner crowd had exploded with the addition of his steak and eggs to the menu. And he would be completely honest with her. He understood she wasn't looking to have her ego stroked but to boost profits and grow her reputation.

When Gia emerged from the back, Savannah was already seated at the large round table Gia considered her family table. She seemed in good enough spirits, laughing at something Trevor said. Maybe she'd just needed a minute of peace to clear her mind. Gia could certainly understand that. She was just glad she seemed to be doing better.

With a sigh, knowing if she didn't stop to say hello to the Bailey sisters they'd simply get up and come to her the instant she sat down to eat in the dining room, Gia stopped by their table. "Hi, Estelle. Esmeralda. How are you today?"

"Doing well, thank you." Estelle gave a quick look around the room. Though the woman was obviously aiming for discretion, she only appeared more suspicious. Then she crooked a finger for Gia to come closer.

Gia indulged her, knowing the sooner she did, the sooner she could escape to her breakfast. Her stomach growled, loudly, as if on cue.

As soon as she leaned down, Esmeralda pounced. "Did you hear about the murder out in Rolling Pines?"

"I did, yes." She rapidly calculated what information would be public knowledge, not wanting to give away any tidbits they didn't already know. "It was across the street from me."

"Oh." Estelle, the more compassionate of the two, though not by much, patted Gia's hand. "I'm so sorry to hear that, sweetie."

"Thank you."

"But I wouldn't worry yourself too much." Esmeralda continued as if there were no interruption. "From what we hear, which came directly from a source who was at the crime scene, Gladys Hoffmeier, that grumbling old windbag . . ."

Gia bit back a smile. No doubt who their source was.

"Was beaten with something." Having delivered her news, Esmeralda sat back and forked up a bit of her veggie omelet, content to let Estelle continue with the specifics.

Estelle broke off a piece of croissant, giving her sister's information time to settle before continuing the story. "But the police already have a suspect in custody."

"They do?" Because that was news to Gia. She whipped out her cell phone, checked her texts in case she'd missed one from Hunt. Nope. Nothing.

"Yes, indeed. Some vagrant they found running from the crime scene."

A stab of guilt shot through Gia, followed by a shiver of fear. Had the man she'd told Hunt about actually been the killer? Had he been standing right there on the street amid a group of unsuspecting civilians staring straight at her? Or had the sisters gotten their information wrong? It was possible, but usually even their bad intel had some basis in truth. Although, this time, Gia had no way to know if her alerting Hunt and him going after the man to question him had prompted the gossip. "Do you know who he is?"

"Carter something or other." Esmeralda waved a hand.

"Marx," Estelle supplied. "Carter Marx. Apparently, he lives out at the far back of the development along the forest border. From what we heard, he and Gladys had more than one run-in over the past few weeks. And the confrontations escalated each time the two ran into each other, according to those in the know, anyway."

Ben had said something similar, that he'd witnessed Carter aim a dirty look at Gladys, though he hadn't mentioned seeing the two of them have words. "Do you know what they were arguing about?"

"No idea. But we will soon enough." Esmeralda lifted her penciled-on eyebrows. "We're going straight to the beauty parlor after we finish our lunch."

Of course they were. Even though both of their blue beehives were in perfect order, not a strand of hair out of place. And from the salon, they'd no doubt hit up every other gossip hot spot in Boggy Creek before the day was through and then start their rounds all over again first thing in the morning.

Gia straightened, more than ready to be done with any talk of murder.

"You know," Esmeralda mused as she dug through her bag, "it's probably for the best, anyway. If Carter hadn't killed her, no doubt her scheming ex-husband would have."

"Sooner rather than later, too," Estelle added. "That woman's been trashing him all over town to anyone who would listen. Supposedly, she had some kind of dirt on him and was going to blow the whistle."

"Said it would ruin his law career and leave his reputation in tatters." Esmeralda nodded knowingly, as if she'd witnessed whatever it was firsthand.

Estelle shrugged. "Maybe it was simply the fact that she caught him cheating with his receptionist."

Esmeralda rolled her eyes. "That stick in the mud couldn't even come up with something original. But rumor had it he was furious with her. He said so right out loud, more than once, in public places—"

"Even if those places were bars." Estelle held up a finger. "And he'd supposedly had more than a few too many at the time."

"Still . . ." Esmeralda waved her off. "Drunk or not, he did threaten bodily harm if he ever got his hands on her. So . . ."

Estelle shrugged and left a few bills on the table for Willow.

"I'll ring you up." Gia took her credit card and went to the register. While she waited for the card to go through, she contemplated the information the sisters had shared. Unfortunately, it didn't leave her with much more than she'd had in the first place. Still, it was something to think about. After a quick round to refill coffees for the few remaining customers, Gia joined her friends at the back table. As she watched the sisters leave, she couldn't help but wonder what the two of them would come up with before tomorrow.

Chapter Seven

Gia filled her plate with sausage and scrambled eggs, scooped on a pile of home fries, and added a drizzle of honey with a sprinkling of cinnamon to a couple pieces of toast. Before biting in, she nodded toward Willow and Skyla. "I just want to thank you guys again for coming in this morning so I could get out to the house when Hunt called."

Willow, who'd been a waitress at the café since she'd opened, waved her off as she bit into a bagel. "You know how much I love working here. I'll come in pretty much any time you need me."

"I do know that, and I can't tell you both how much I appreciate it." It was comforting to know she'd have backup whenever the need arose.

Skyla, with the same petite build as Willow's, the same long, dark hair, and the same exotic green eyes, could easily pass for the young girl's sister rather than her mother. "Probably as much as we appreciate how good you are to both of us."

Gia couldn't help but smile. After the long night she'd spent unable to sleep, and the morning's events, it was good to relax with friends.

"So, what did the Bailey sisters have to say?" Savannah dug into her pancakes with gusto, apparently over whatever mood had gripped her earlier.

Gia shrugged, chewed a bite of toast, and washed it down with much-needed caffeine. "Not much, for them, anyway."

"It's early yet," Cole put in.

A quick look around assured her no one in the café seemed interested in their conversation. Still, she leaned forward as she spoke and kept her voice low. "They did say Gladys was beaten," which she'd already known from Hunt, "and that the police have a suspect in custody." Considering they had the first half right, she could only assume the second part was accurate as well.

Everyone paused, most with forks halfway to their mouths, and waited for her to elaborate.

"I don't know if I'm buying it, though. It seems way too soon." Gia forked up a bit of sausage and scrambled eggs, savored for a moment, then swallowed. "They also said the guy that was arrested was, and I quote, some vagrant named Carter Marx. Ben mentioned him yesterday too. Does anyone know him?"

"Yeah." Cole pointed with his fork. "He lives out at the back of the property. As far as I know, there's no house back there. He probably towed in a trailer or pitched a tent."

"I thought that wasn't allowed in Rolling Pines. Isn't that why they claim they charge HOA fees?" Which weren't as high as in some developments, but still . . .

He shrugged. "Far as I know, several people do the same. With over a thousand acres of property out there, more than half of it undeveloped, plus more than six hundred square miles of forest bordering the development on three sides, there's no way to police it all."

"Huh." The memory of the man running from the scene came back to her. If he was Carter Marx, maybe he'd simply run because of the extensive police presence. He might have not wanted to get caught squatting. "Do you know what Carter looks like?"

"Sure. Tall, lanky fellow with long, dark hair that hangs down about mid-back." He reached behind himself to point to a spot on his Hawaiian-print shirt a good twelve inches past where his own shaggy salt-and-pepper hair curled over his collar. "Uh . . . what else? Usually has on ripped, dirty-looking jeans, sandals that have seen better days, and a penchant for army green. Walks his pit bull through the neighborhood all the time."

With such a vivid description, there was no doubt in Gia's mind he was the man who'd taken off from the crime scene, the suspect Hunt currently had in custody, if the Bailey sisters were to be believed. "Ben Stettler said he saw Carter walking his dog past Gladys the other day when she was outside getting the mail, and he gave her a dirty look."

"Hmm. Never seen him do that before. He usually keeps his head down, or offers a quick half wave." Cole wiped his mouth and tossed his napkin onto his empty plate, then set it aside on the cutout above him and pulled his coffee in front of him on the place mat. "You know who you should ask is Harley. Seems I've seen the two of them together a time or two out at the park."

"Maybe I'll hang around for a bit after I set his dinner up out back tonight and see if he comes around early." She'd been leaving the homeless man's dinner on a table she'd set up behind the café since the first time she'd found him in the back parking lot foraging in her dumpster. Not only was Harley a sweetheart, he'd also saved Savannah's life. And he'd become a very close friend to both Gia and Savannah. Especially once he'd gotten to know them and moved past some of his shyness. He'd even walked inside a building, which Harley never, ever did, to save Gia once.

"Actually . . ." Since Earl had eaten his usual hardy breakfast earlier, he simply picked at a muffin and nursed a mug of coffee. "I saw him on my way in, and he said to let you know Donna Mae was going to eat with him tonight. Sorry. With all the hullabaloo this morning, I forgot to pass on the message."

"No problem." Donna Mae Parker and Harley had recently reconnected, having lost track of each other in the years after they'd been high school sweethearts. Donna Mae owned a local flower shop and had become a fast friend of Gia's. Gia would think of something a little special to set out for them, maybe put a couple of candles on the table.

The front door opened and a group of teenagers bopped in, laughing and roughhousing.

So much for finishing breakfast. Gia sighed and started to stand.

Willow popped up. "I'll take care of them. I'm done eating. You go ahead and finish up."

Cole took Willow's plate and set it next to his own. "And I'm on the grill. So, you two ladies relax and finish your breakfast."

Earl and Skyla stood as well, clearing more plates and empty mugs. Earl grabbed the coffeepot from behind the counter and topped off Gia's and Savannah's. When he held the pot up to Alfie, he splayed a hand over his mostly empty mug. "Thanks, anyway, Earl, but I've got to get going. I have a ton of work piling up."

"Are you going to be around later?" Gia asked.

He grinned. "I'll tell you what. If you're up for it, I'll bring dinner tonight. I'll even bring enough for Hunt and Leo if they show up. If not, they can always heat it up whenever they can take a break. What sounds good? Mexican, maybe?"

"Ugh." Savannah groaned and clutched her stomach. "No way. Not after the amount of food I just consumed. How about something lighter?"

"Salads?" Alfie offered.

"Don't get all crazy now, not that light," she said and laughed. "How about we'll text you later and let you know what we're in the mood for. But I feel like it will definitely involve French fries."

"Sounds good to me." Alfie popped up from his seat. "I'm always up for French fries. They're pretty much the perfect food."

Not that he was wrong, but grease and salt weren't typically Savannah's style.

When the front door opened again, Alfie gave them a two-finger salute. "I'll catch you guys later."

Savannah leaned forward. "Don't turn around and look, but do you know who just walked in?"

Gia started to turn, because what else would you do when someone says don't look? Then she caught herself. "Who?"

"Miley Davis. And, if I'm not mistaken, she's with Scott Hoffmeier."

"Gladys's husband?"

"*Ex*-husband," Savannah reminded. Then she jumped up, leaned close to Gia's ear on her way past, and whispered, "Sit tight."

Gia turned as if looking after her and took the opportunity to check out Miley and Scott.

Scott was about average height and average build, with short brown hair and muddy brown eyes. He wore tan Dockers, brown boat shoes, and a pale yellow polo shirt. When Savannah greeted them with menus and a megawatt smile, he lowered his gaze and softly thanked her. Everything about him screamed guy next door. Gia had a hard time imagining him married to the outgoing, to put it kindly, Gladys.

Miley, on the other hand, while just as soft-spoken, as Gia knew from the few occasions she'd run into her by the house, was stunning. Auburn hair hung in loose waves over her delicate shoulders and down her back. Emerald eyes that tilted up slightly at the corners lent her a feline look, as did the smooth way she carried herself. With her stylish hunter green dress, neck and wrists adorned with delicate gold, and pearls at her ears, the woman could easily have just stepped off a New York or Paris runway. To think the short, squatty Gladys, with her red curls packed in tight against her head, was related, never mind a sister, to the tall, curvy Miley was surprising enough. But the biggest difference between the two was their dispositions. Where Gladys was nasty, sarcastic, and outright mean, Miley was kind, quiet, and personable.

When Savannah started straight toward her, Gia stood. She waited while Savannah seated the pair at the table next to theirs, then went to offer her condolences. Before either of them sat, she shook both of their hands. "I'm so sorry for your loss."

"Thank you," Scott said quietly, his gaze riveted on his shoes.

Miley thanked her, as well, then waited until Scott had pulled out her chair to sit.

Not knowing what else to say, and with neither of them offering to make conversation, Gia tipped her head. "Well, then, I hope you enjoy your breakfast."

Miley offered a killer smile and thanked her again, while Scott buried his face in the menu.

When Gia returned to her seat, Savannah grabbed her coffee and sat next to her, with her back to Scott and Miley. When she aimed her Cheshire cat grin at Gia, she had no doubt why she'd jumped up to seat the two right next to their table.

Gia lowered her gaze and shook her head, then sipped her coffee to cover the smile playing at the corners of her mouth. At least Savannah was back to her mischievous self.

"So, are you ever going to marry my cousin, or are you two just going to stay engaged forever?" Savannah eyed her over the top of her mug.

Gia nearly spit out her coffee, managed to choke it down, then glared. "You did that on purpose, waited for me to have a mouthful of coffee."

Savannah offered a coy smile. "Maybe."

"Smart aleck."

"Yup. But I'm ready to plan a wedding, and I want you to have . . . uh . . ." She pressed a finger against her lips, rested her elbow on her chair back, and tilted her head.

Gia lowered her head until she caught Scott in her peripheral vision and turned her ear to whatever conversation between Scott and Miley had caught Savannah's attention. When it came to eaves-dropping, Savannah was a pro. It didn't matter if she was completely engrossed in a conversation, she could always pick up what was happening around her. And the fact that she'd stopped mid-sentence while trying to cajole Gia into a shotgun wedding meant she'd overheard something juicy. Gia strained to hear the quiet conversation.

Scott slammed his menu down on the table with enough force to rattle the silverware.

Gia jumped but refrained from turning and giving them reason to lower their voices even further.

"I already told you," Scott said between gritted teeth, "I wasn't cheating on Gladys. She walked in when I was hugging my receptionist and jumped to conclusions. Just like she always did."

"And why were you hugging another woman?" Miley asked with a sarcastic bite.

He slumped with a sigh. "She'd just found out her husband was hurt at work, badly. I gave her a hug, told her how sorry I was, and asked her if she needed a ride to the hospital. That's all."

"Well, that's not how Gladys told it," Miley said. "And, regardless, it doesn't matter anyway. She divorced you six months ago and had already changed her will."

Scott's face turned beet red. "I'm not having this discussion with you again. You know that inheritance is mine."

"Not anymore, Scott. And being a lawyer, you should know that, which you clearly do. If you had any other recourse, you wouldn't be here harassing me." Miley took a deep breath, seemed to regain her composure, and sighed. "Look, let's just enjoy lunch, and we can air our grievances later, somewhere more private."

Gia barely resisted the urge to squirm as her gaze met Savannah's.

"I said it before, and I'll say it again . . ." Scott started calmly. "All you have to do is turn everything over to me, as it should have been left in the first place. Most of that money's mine, anyway, and you know it."

Miley maintained perfect control. "Sorry, Scott, but when you pay for a service, the money no longer belongs to you."

He ground his teeth together so hard they were in danger of shattering. "If I had known she was going to change her will, I would have—"

Miley slammed her palms against the table and shoved to her feet. Her chair tipped behind her. "You'd have what? Not paid her? Not killed her?"

This time, Gia did turn and stared right at Scott, as did everyone else in the thankfully almost empty dining room. Even Cole poked his head through the cutout from the kitchen, where he was preparing their order. He frowned at Gia. "Is everything okay out there?"

Scott's face turned ten more shades of red before finally settling on one that bordered purple. "Everything is fine. I'm sorry for the fuss."

Miley righted her chair, returned to her seat, and laid her napkin across her lap. "Sit down, Scott."

"No thanks. I'd rather dine with a barracuda." He started for the door, then paused and tossed back over his shoulder, "Oh, wait, I was already dining with a shark."

Miley sighed and sipped her coffee, pointedly ignoring any lingering stares. Then she took out her phone and immersed herself in something Gia couldn't see on the screen, not for lack of trying.

With the drama over, Gia and Savannah stood and started clearing the rest of their own table. Once they'd finished, Gia grabbed Miley's order from the cutout and set it on her table. She left Scott's plate where it was. "Can I get you anything else? More coffee, maybe?"

"No, thank you, Gia. I'm sorry for the commotion with Scott." She gestured in the direction he'd gone.

"Don't even worry about it. It's not your fault." But sadly, it would fuel the rumor mill until something juicier came along. And something more interesting than a murder accusation against a victim's ex-husband by her sister would be pretty hard to come by. "And I apologize. Scott had me so frazzled even before we came in that I forgot my manners. I actually stopped by because I wanted to thank you."

"Thank me?" Gia shook her perfectly manicured, proffered hand. "For what?"

"Asking the police to do a welfare check on my sister when you found that video. I know how Gladys treated you, and I heard about what she threatened to do to Thor, and I cannot tell you how sorry I am for that."

"Again, it's not your fault. Gladys was . . ." She searched for a word of kindness for Gladys's grieving sister, which suddenly made her realize Scott didn't seem to be at all grief-stricken. Even if they were divorced, she'd have expected some sort of sympathy from a man who'd shared at least some part of his life with her, had presumably loved her at one time. When Gia's ex had been killed, she'd battled all sorts of emotions, including grief, and that man had cheated on her, conned tons of people, including close friends and clients, and nearly landed her in prison just because she'd been associated with him. Of course, his body had been found in her dumpster and she'd been the prime suspect, so there was also that. "She seemed unhappy. And I'm sorry for that. No one should go through life that way."

"You're right. Sadly, my sister had a difficult life. She was bitter, jealous, angry, and she didn't like to go without. Finding Scott in another woman's arms nearly sent her over the edge." She shrugged one slim shoulder. "Scott had always taken care of Gladys, and I was worried when she divorced him and moved in with me that she'd stay indefinitely."

Gia didn't know how to respond to that, since she'd harbored the same concern.

"Oh, trust me, I know it sounds awful under the circumstances, but it was true. She'd made it seem like Scott had tossed her out with nothing, and I took her in for free, out of the goodness of my heart. And do you know how she repaid me?" She sucked in a deep breath, regained her composure and smiled, then waved away whatever she'd been about to blurt in a fit of anger. "None of that matters now. Water under the bridge, as they say. It doesn't even matter that she lied to get me to feel sorry for her. But then I came across the paperwork she'd left out and discovered she'd stashed away quite a nest egg and had planned to build her own house in Rolling Pines. She even bought a piece of property along the back."

"Oh, really? I hadn't heard that." The spark of relief that Gladys would not be a permanent resident of Rolling Pines brought a tidal wave of guilt. Surely, it would have been fine if she'd lived at the back of the development, away from Gia's house. Either way, she still wouldn't have wanted to see her dead, even if it did mean putting up with her accusations and threats. Gia could always have moved.

Miley slid her untouched plate away, stood, and retrieved her purse. "Yes, well, too bad she didn't find out Carter Marx was squatting on the land before she bought it. That might have saved everyone a lot of grief."

Chapter Eight

Gia tossed her apron into the hamper in the hallway closet, pushed through the door to the café kitchen, and inhaled deeply. The scent of pasta, cheese, and Italian seasoning, plus the sausage and ground beef Savannah had added to the two trays of lasagna she was just taking out of the oven, had her mouth watering. "This was really nice of you to do for Harley and Donna Mae."

"You locked up already?" Balancing a tray on two oven mitts, she nodded toward a trivet on the counter by the sink.

Gia grabbed it and set it on the center island. "Yup. All done. You're sure you don't just want to eat here, right? Thor is going to bounce around the car all the way home when he gets in and smells this."

Savannah laughed. At some point during the day, she decided she felt like having Italian food for dinner. She'd texted Alfie, who then ran to the supermarket and brought her everything she needed to make lasagna. "Nah. I want to get these shoes off, sit somewhere comfortable, and eat.

No way would Gia argue with her, considering Savannah's lasagna was the best she'd ever tasted. And it would be even better at home in her comfiest pajamas. "The table outside is set. I used the checkered tablecloth, and put the flowers Alfie brought in a vase, then put out a couple of candles and left a lighter on the table."

Savannah set the tray on the trivet. "You're sure it's okay to leave the whole tray? It's not like Harley has a refrigerator to put the leftovers in."

"Donna Mae does, so she can take them home if she wants, but I also gave her a key to the back door a while back, just in case they ever needed anything."

Savannah nodded, licked sauce off her thumb, then rolled her eyes. "Amazing, if I do say so myself."

"It always is."

Savannah removed her apron, yanked out her scrunchie, and shook her hair out. Then she washed and dried her hands. "Oh, hey, Leo and Hunt are sure to work late tonight. You want to make some popcorn and watch an old movie like we used to do in New York?"

"I'd love that. Did you have anything special in mind?"

"Nah, whatever's streaming." She lifted one of the trays. "Could you get the back door?"

"Sure thing." Gia pushed the back door open and held it for Savannah to set the lasagna on the table and check that everything was just perfect. A bottle of wine sat in an ice bucket, plates and silverware were set out, along with water and wineglasses. The immediate surroundings, a parking lot lined along the back by dumpsters for each of the businesses, didn't boast much of a view. But the wooded area beyond the lot was thick with moss-covered oaks and pine trees.

"Oh, hey," Savannah said. "Could you grab a spatula and the pitcher of ice water from the fridge?"

"You bet." As Gia started back inside, Donna Mae pulled into the back lot.

Hoping she'd get to chat for a few minutes before Harley arrived and she and Savannah made themselves scarce, Gia made quick work of the chore. When she returned, Donna Mae was already chatting with Savannah. She turned to Gia and gave her a quick cheek kiss. "Everything looks wonderful. Thank you so much for doing this."

"Any time, you know that. But I can't take credit. This time, it was all Savannah."

"Well, thank you, Savannah." When she tipped her head, a mass of blonde curls shifted in front of her eyes. She shook them back.

"You're very welcome. I hope you enjoy it." She smiled warmly, then gestured across the lot. "Here comes Harley now."

Harley limped across the lot in his usual stilted gait. As always, he took his time. He tended to savor every moment rather than rushing through whatever he was doing and moving on to the next thing. Maybe she could learn a thing or two from him. When he reached the table, he nodded to both Gia and Savannah and smiled shyly at Donna Mae.

"Nice." Which was the equivalent of jubilation for Harley, who was a man of few words.

"Sit, relax." Gia pulled out a chair for Donna Mae, and Harley took his seat across from her. "Harley, do you mind if I ask you a quick question before I get out of your hair?"

He kept his hands in his lap and shrugged.

"Do you know a guy named Carter Marx? He lives out by me in Rolling Pines."

"He don't live nowhere."

"So, he is squatting on land out there?"

"Has a tent for him and his dog. Moves it if anyone comes. Moves around the land anyway every few days if they don't."

Knowing that was about as much as she was likely to get out of him, and that was quite a bit compared to his usual one-word answers, she considered the most important information she was looking for. She'd already confirmed Carter was homeless and squatting on land that apparently belonged to Gladys. So, how could she get Harley to sum up what she needed to know in a few words? "Two more questions, okay?"

He nodded once.

"Did he ever mention Gladys Hoffmeier to you?"

"Yup."

She waited, but there was nothing more forthcoming. Great, now she'd have to ask him to elaborate, and that would have to be her second question. "What did he say about her?"

"She's mean."

Gia resisted the urge to push any further. She loved Harley dearly and would never do anything to make him uncomfortable, which continuing to interrogate him would. Plus, she'd learned her lesson the hard way not to involve him in any investigations she got caught up in. He'd already been hurt because of her. "Thank you, Harley. That was a big help, and I truly appreciate it."

He shrugged and beamed at her. "Sure."

"You guys enjoy your dinner."

"Thank you." Harley's gaze skittered across the table. Although Gia had offered numerous times to leave breakfast for him too, he'd always refused to take more than one meal from her. And it had been difficult enough for her to convince him to accept that much. In exchange, he chose to keep an eye on the café for her when she was closed. A kindness that had come in handy more than once and saved Savannah's life.

She and Savannah said good night, then started back inside, but Savannah turned back. "Harley?"

"Yeah."

"Do you like Carter Marx?"

"Nope."

"Thanks, sweetie."

He blushed all the way to the roots of his more gray than blonde hair. "Uh-huh."

"Brilliant," Gia said as she closed and locked the door behind them.

"Harley's a great judge of character. He likes most everyone, but when he doesn't, you can be sure there's a good reason." Savannah started toward Gia's office. She checked her hair in the mirror, made a few adjustments to her part.

Gia marveled that even after a long day, Savannah always managed to appear completely put together. What little makeup she wore looked freshly applied, her hair, which had been up all day, hung in loose waves, and a pink glow tinged her cheeks. "Yeah, but no way am I pushing him to explain. I'm already worried that I even mentioned Carter to him. Now he's sure to keep an eye on him at the least."

"He'll be okay." Savannah grabbed her purse from the desk drawer and handed it to Gia, then headed for the kitchen and picked up the tray of lasagna. "He's not out by Rolling Pines all that often, and I doubt Carter walks the twenty or so miles to the park Harley likes to hang out in on a regular basis, especially in the summer."

"True enough, I guess. Unless he gets spooked because Hunt grabbed him and decides to abandon Rolling Pines." Gia hefted her own bag over her shoulder along with Savannah's as they started out, took one more look around the dining room, then switched off the lights and held the front door open for Savannah. "You want to take one car, and we can ride in together in the morning?"

"Sure. May as well. Is it okay if I stay over tonight?"

"Of course."

"Do you mind stopping to pick up Pepper?"

"Not at all. I'll get Thor, then we'll swing by your house, and you can get together an overnight bag and pick up Pepper." Klondike would be thrilled to have her sister, Savannah's gray and white tabby, to play with.

"Sounds perfect. Without knowing if there's a killer running around out there, I don't want to spend the night alone if Leo can't make it home."

"No, I don't blame you. Even with Thor, I'd prefer having someone around tonight too." Plus, she always enjoyed Savannah's company and missed having her as a full-time roommate.

They loaded the lasagna into the trunk so there'd still be some left by the time they got home, then stopped down the road to pick up Thor. Gia left the air-conditioning running for Savannah, who wanted to wait in the car to text Leo, and ran inside. Since no one was manning the front desk, she called out a quick "Hello."

"Hey, Gia, be right out," Zoe yelled back.

Gia waited, searching through a few brochures on a variety of training classes available. Thankfully, Thor was already extremely well-behaved, mostly thanks to Zoe. He'd been Gia's first pet, and she hadn't had a clue what to do with him other than love him with all of her heart. That part came naturally.

"Hey, sorry." Zoe pushed through the door with Thor at her side.

He bolted to Gia, tail wagging wildly, jumped up and put his paws against her shoulders, then licked her cheek.

So, he was mostly well-behaved. She laughed out loud, a moment of pure joy in what had been a stress-filled day. She dug her fingers in the thick fur around his neck and scratched. "Okay, Thor, I missed you too. Yes, baby, Mommy loves you."

"You know . . ." Zoe grabbed Thor's leash from a hook on the wall. "If I didn't know any better, I'd honestly believe this dog could tell time. Every day, when it's just about time for you to pick him up, he gets restless and starts pacing by the door."

"Aww, baby." Gia hugged him tight.

When the front door opened, Thor dropped to the floor and rushed to greet Trevor.

"Hey, Trevor." Gia frowned at the clock over the desk. "You're closing early."

"Oh, hey. I'm glad I caught you." He finished petting Thor, then straightened. "I just wanted to make sure you knew they released Carter Marx."

"Oh?" Funny, she hadn't heard from Hunt, and she expected he'd have at least texted if he knew anything. Then again, why would he text her that they released Carter when he'd never let her know they'd picked him up in the first place? They were going to have to discuss better communication. Of course, she didn't let him know everything she did all day long either. So, she supposed it was a stalemate.

"Supposedly," Trevor rushed on, "and this is just a rumor, Hunt brought him in for questioning when he fled the crime scene, but they had no evidence that put him at Gladys's anywhere near the time of the murder."

"Great." Dejected, more concerned now that there might be a killer roaming around her home, she sulked.

"But I hear there's a new suspect already," he continued.

That piqued her interest. "Oh, yeah? Who?"

He lifted a brow at her. "Scott Hoffmeier."

"Oh, right." With the news that Carter, whom Harley didn't like, had been released, she'd forgotten all about Scott. She updated Trevor and Zoe about his and Miley's conversation in the café.

"That's a shame." Trevor leaned an elbow on the high counter and crossed one ankle over the other. "I don't know Miley well, but I run into her every now and again, and she comes into Storm Scoopers often enough, and she always seemed so sweet. She didn't deserve to have her own sister—"

"Half sister," Gia and Zoe blurted in unison.

"Right." He grinned. "Half sister. She didn't deserve to have Gladys take advantage of her. Plus, cheat with her husband."

"Whoa! Wait. What?" That was a new one on Gia. How had she missed that doozy? Seemed the Bailey sisters might be slipping. Savannah was going to regret waiting in the car.

"No lie." He nodded eagerly, like a bobblehead on steroids. "According to a woman who lives out there, Gladys and Miley's husband were going at it hot and heavy in the backyard one day."

"Did Miley know?" And if she did, would it be enough motive to kill her own sister?

Trevor shrugged. "Katie didn't know, just that she saw them in a heated embrace while she was vacuuming her pool one afternoon."

"Huh." Because what else could she say? "So, she conned her sis—half sister into taking her in, freeloaded off her, then kissed her husband after she'd been cheated on by her own husband and should have known how it felt to be betrayed."

"That about sums it up." Trevor nodded once, flopping a too-long clump of hair into his eyes.

Chapter Nine

Gia unlocked her front door, shoved it open, and set Pepper down on the floor.

The little cat took off, pounced on Klondike, who'd just come into the foyer to see what was what, and the two tumbled across the floor in a ball of fur.

Gia laughed. It felt amazing to be home. That joy turned tense a moment later, though, when she remembered there might be a killer lurking in the shadows. And she'd left Savannah in the car with Thor. She hurried back down the walkway, scanning every shadow as she went. Even with Gladys no longer posing a threat, she didn't feel comfortable letting Thor out off his leash. Who knew? Maybe she never would.

"Hey, boy. Sorry about that." She clipped Thor's leash to his collar while Savannah got the lasagna from the trunk.

Just as they started for the house, Alfie pulled up and tooted the horn of his blue MINI Cooper. He parked along the side of the road, jumped out, and jogged across the lawn. "Hey, you guys need me to grab anything?"

"You want to take Thor so I can get our bags?" Gia held the leash out to him. When he reached for it, she hesitated. "Make sure you hold him tight."

"I will. Promise." He squatted beside Thor and gave him a vigorous rubdown while he waited for her to get what she needed and lock the car.

"Okay, we're all set." Anxious to get Thor inside, Gia rushed to the door and held it open for Savannah, Alfie, and Thor to precede her. The instant they made it into the foyer, she slammed the door shut and turned the dead bolt. She dropped hers and Savannah's purses, along with Savannah's overnight bag, in the foyer to deal with later. Right now, she was starved. Since Zoe had already fed Thor, all she had to do was feed the cats, wash her hands, and set the table.

"I'm already feeding the cats," Savannah called from the kitchen. "I'll just be a minute, if you want to set the table."

Even better, one less chore to do. Gia found her by the laundry room off the kitchen, filling bowls with water and cat food. "You want to eat in here or in the living room?"

"Doesn't matter." The instant Savannah finished filling the bowls, the two felines unwound themselves from her feet in favor of their meals.

Savannah toed off heels Gia had no clue how she walked in all day, washed her hands and dropped onto a chair at the kitchen table. "I'm beat."

Gia followed suit. "Me too."

Alfie washed his hands, grabbed diet sodas from the fridge and started setting the table. "Not me. I'm revved. I finished my job early, beat the deadline by at least a few hours, and even ended up with some time to devote to research."

"Oh?" That perked Gia right up, considering the only research Alfie would have been doing would involve Gladys's murder. Gia took a minute to catch him up on what she'd heard throughout the day while she popped a loaf of frozen garlic bread into the oven.

"Do you have salad fixings in the fridge?" Savannah pulled the door open and began to rummage through what little Gia kept in the refrigerator, which was mostly drinks—sweet tea, soda, water, and orange juice that might or might not be past the expiration date, since they'd finished off the fresh-squeezed pitcher.

"I think so. I know there's lettuce." Other than that, it was a toss-up. She didn't often shop for home. When she worked in a café all day long and fast food was easy enough to pick up if she wanted something different, what was the point?

When Gia turned around, Alfie had the table set and was already scrolling through his phone. "I'll pull this up on the computer later, but I wanted you to see it early in case you wanted to try to get hold of Irene before dark."

"Why would I want to do that?" Although, she had considered speaking to the head of the HOA, get her take on Gladys. Plus, if anything went on in Rolling Pines, Irene should know about it. Such as, how had Carter Marx pitching a tent in the development gone unnoticed when it was expressly forbidden in the lengthy list of rules Gia had studied when she'd first moved in?

"Because Irene paid Gladys a visit after she came by to harass you about Thor and before she was killed." Alfie held his phone out so she could see the screen and hit Play. An image of Gia's yard from Miley's front door came into focus.

Gia squinted and leaned closer to the phone. "How'd you get this video?"

Savannah squished against her to watch. "What are we looking for?"

He yanked at his collar. "Okay, so, I might have hacked into her doorbell camera. Okay. Wait for it."

Gia didn't bother reprimanding him. What would be the point? A moment later, a car pulled alongside the front of Miley's yard. Irene Kellerman got out and looked around, then smoothed her peach suit skirt, straightened her pearls, and lifted her chin. Then she hurried across the lawn to the front door.

Before she even reached it, the door swung open, and Gladys stepped out onto the front porch.

The view wasn't great, especially on such a small screen. While she could make out the two women standing face-to-face, she couldn't get a feel for the mood. "Is there any sound?"

"Nope. Just the video." Alfie craned his neck to see the screen then held up a finger. "Here. Watch their hands. Closely."

Gia did as he said. Gladys turned and reached into the house, then jotted something on a notepad, ripped off the page, and shoved it into Irene's hands. There was no mistaking the anger when she tossed the pad and pen aside on a small round table on the porch that sat between two rocking chairs and propped her hands on her hips.

Irene scowled at the page in her hand.

Then Gladys pointed toward the street.

With a last parting shot that Gia couldn't hear, Irene spun on her heel and stormed off.

"Can you rewind it? Maybe we can read her lips?"

Alfie was already shaking his head. "I tried on the computer, even tried blowing it up, but the camera angle is off. You can't make out what she's saying."

"Did my cameras pick up anything?" She started to reach for her phone.

"Nope, this took place earlier, when I ran out for what I'd need to install the cameras."

"And I stayed inside with Thor." Which meant there was no way to know what had gone on outside between Gladys coming over and the time Alfie set up her app that evening. Gia looked around the kitchen.

Before she could make up her mind what to do next, Savannah bumped Gia's shoulder with her own. "Go. I'll get the salad together, keep an eye on the garlic bread, and put the lasagna in the oven to warm. Alfie will work his magic on the video."

"And see if I can find out when Gladys purchased the land," he added, already digging through his bag and pulling out his laptop.

"And you go see if you can find Irene," Savannah said. "With Gladys's side facing the camera, and the bad angle on Irene's mouth, the only way we're going to find out what they said to each other is to ask."

"And even then, there's no guarantee she's going to tell me the truth." But Gia ran back through what they'd been able to see of the interaction. "It seemed to me like they were arguing."

"Yeah, I'd say." Alfie moved a plate aside to give himself room for the laptop. "That's definitely the impression I got, and I've already watched it several times on the larger screen."

"All right. Lock the door behind me, and I'll take a quick run down to the Homeowners Association office and see if Irene's still there." Since events were often held after hours, there was a good chance Irene would still be around. She wished she had an excuse to drop by, but she'd already paid her dues for the month. Still, when her neighbor had been murdered right across the street, it seemed reasonable she'd want to talk to the head of the HOA. At least, it did to Gia.

It took less than five minutes for her to drive down to the front of the development, swing through the parking lot and pull up in front of the small office. Even though she could clearly see the *Closed* sign displayed in the window, she got out of the car, walked up the wooden ramp and peered inside. Dark. She knocked, waited, knocked again, then finally gave up and headed back to her car. She'd have to try on her way home after work tomorrow, since there was no way Irene would be up and in the office as early as Gia left.

Disappointed, Gia headed back home. She parked in the driveway, got out and locked up, then started up the walkway. She couldn't help her attention being drawn to Miley's. It seemed no one was home.

Considering the crime scene tape still stretched around the property, she wouldn't be surprised if Miley and her husband, Elijah, if memory served, were staying elsewhere. *If* they were even still together, if what Trevor's source had told him was correct. When she started to look away, she noticed Ben Stettler's garage door standing open.

Ben, who'd been working in his front yard the day Gladys had come over to berate Gia about Thor. Could he have still been there when Irene had visited Gladys? Would he have heard whatever went on between the two? He'd noticed Gladys come over to Gia's. So, maybe . . .

She changed direction and started toward Ben's. Thankfully, the sun set late in the summer, but shadows had already begun to creep over the forest. It would be full dark soon, and no way did she want to get caught outside after dark. Even if the killer wasn't lurking nearby, plenty of other things might be.

She crossed the street and looked around as she walked up Ben's driveway toward his farmhouse-style home. The house where Gladys had lived, the only two-story house on the block, looked dark, empty, foreboding. Gia shifted her gaze away. When she reached Ben's two-car garage, she looked inside. No sign of Ben. "Ben? You around?"

The back door stood open as well, and Gia started through the garage toward it. She skirted an old pickup truck with its hood up and squeezed between it and what appeared to be a homemade tool bench, every square inch of it covered in tools, boxes of nails and screws, shop rags, even a few stained paint cans. While Ben kept his yard immaculate, it seemed his sense of order didn't carry through to the garage. When she finally reached the back door, she poked her head out. "Ben? You out here?"

"Gia? That you?" He peered from the open door of a shed, rag in hand, wiping some sort of metal. "Hold up. I'll be right there."

With bushes on either side of her thick enough to conceal anything from a spider the size of her hand—a chill rushed through her—to an armadillo, Gia stepped back inside the garage to wait for him. She browsed while she waited, amazed at the sheer number of tools. Her own garage contained a hammer, two screwdrivers, a gardening shovel she'd yet to use, and a roll and a half of duct tape.

On the rare occasion she needed something else, she usually borrowed it from Savannah or Hunt.

She picked up some kind of prickly, circular wire brush with a piece sticking up out of it where you could attach it to something, and wondered what on earth you'd attach it to and what you'd do with it once you did. The idea of having to spend the evening in the ER for a tetanus shot rather than settling in with good food and great friends had her dropping it back amid the mess. She brushed off her hands and turned to see if Ben was coming.

Darkness had already fallen and light spilled from the shed, bathing the lawn in its glow but deepening the shadows surrounding the yard, which had her second-guessing her decision. She'd wait another minute or two, but then she was leaving. She could always come back tomorrow.

She paced the back of the garage, scanning the shelves. When her gaze fell on a hammer sitting on the tool bench, she smiled. At least he had some tools she recognized. Then she noted the smudge of red marring the middle of the well-worn wood handle. She leaned closer, studied the mark, let her gaze follow it up along the handle to the metal top, where a dark stain she couldn't make out marred the flaked metal. Esmeralda's words came screaming back—*she was beaten with something*—begging her to get out of there.

"Oh, hey, there you are. I was just . . ."

Gia whirled toward the sound of Ben's voice.

He held a red rag in one hand and was cleaning what looked like grease off his other hand. The hand holding the rag was wrapped in a bandage that wound around his knuckles and thumb and up to his wrist. Sweat soaked her back. She needed to get out of there, had to make sure Savannah and Alfie were safely locked inside with Thor, Klondike, and Pepper . . . She had to call Hunt.

"Trying to fix the lawnmower. That thing's always busted. I guess I'm going to have to break down and invest in a new one, because no way am I mowing an acre of land with a push mower every week. I am way too old for that nonsense." He finally looked up, tossed the rag onto the tool bench, and smiled. "So, to what do I owe the pleasure of a lovely lady's company this fine evening?"

"I-I-I uh-uh-uh . . ."

Ben laughed. "Cat got your tongue, girl?"

She tried for a smile, may have ended up with a grimace. "Sorry, I uh . . ."

"Right, you said that already."

She shook her head, suppressed a shiver, and forced a smile. "I'm sorry. You s-startled me. I guess I'm just jumpy."

His smile faltered. "Ah, man, I'm sorry, Gia. I didn't even think with what happened to Gladys that you'd be on edge. Forgive me."

"No problem." She waved him off. "That's actually why I stopped by. I wanted to ask you about that day."

"Sure, shoot." He leaned a hip against the tool bench and folded his arms across his chest, then winced, glanced at his injured hand, and resettled himself more timidly.

"What'd you do to your hand?" The words were out before she could censor them. No wonder Hunt was always annoyed with her for inserting herself in his investigations. It seemed she couldn't help herself even when she wasn't trying to be nosy.

He gestured toward the hammer and grinned. "I didn't get my thumb out of the way in time."

"Did you have it looked at?"

"Nah. It's fine." He waved her off. "Trust me when I tell you, there's not a project around here that doesn't have some trace of my DNA on it. Occupational hazard. So, how can I help you?"

Gia tried to refocus her attention. If Ben Stettler was a killer, and had beaten Gladys to death with his hands or the hammer, he sure was cool about it, dismissing her concerns so offhandedly. Either way, she'd let Hunt know. But, in the meantime, while she was there, she may as well ask what she'd come to find out. Besides, if she took off running, she'd only alert him to her suspicions. Although, she wasn't about to stand there in the back of his garage with a pickup truck between her and anyone's view inside. Not that there was anyone around the deserted neighborhood, but still . . .

"Um. So, a few hours after Gladys came over to my house, she received a visit from Irene Kellerman. Did you see her come by?" She started to stroll casually around the truck as she spoke, leaving him to trail after her.

He followed. "Sure. I was still out front working on the sprinklers. Why?"

When she reached the open garage door, she breathed a sigh of relief. Foolish to be so jumpy, but it did tell her she should probably back off and let Hunt do the investigating. Which she would—right after she spoke to Ben. "It looked like they were having some kind of argument, and I was just wondering what it was about."

"Hmm. I don't remember hearing any argument. I just saw Irene walk across the front yard and up onto the porch. After that, I minded my own business. I assume she was there to go over the list of violations Miley hadn't yet seen to." He scowled, scratched his head with his unbandaged hand. "I suppose they could have been arguing over that. I overheard Gladys and Miley arguing over the work that needed to be done—painting the mailbox and trimming the hedges—not that long ago. Then again, Gladys would argue over anything. She and Irene could just as well have been fighting about whether the sky was blue."

Since Gia couldn't argue with his assessment, and couldn't think of anything else to ask, she simply nodded.

Ben frowned. "You don't think Irene could have had anything to do with her death, do you?"

Did she? She couldn't imagine the demure woman, with her skirts, high heels, and delicate jewelry, beating anyone. Then again, Gladys had nearly pushed Gia into taking a swing. So, there was that. "No. I just saw she was there and they seemed to be arguing, so I wondered what it was about. That's all. Just my curiosity getting the better of me."

"Can I give you a word of advice?" He offered a kind smile.

"Sure."

"Keep to yourself and don't go asking around about Gladys."

"I-uh—"

"That woman was nothing but trouble. Now, I'm not saying she deserved what happened to her, mind you. No one deserves that, and I am a peace-loving man, and I don't like to see any creature come to harm, but that woman racked up enemies like roadkill attracts flies."

"I—"

"The best thing you can do is go home, tend to your pets, and let the police investigate Gladys's murder. If you ask me, which you sort of did, Gladys was specifically targeted. What happened to her seems personal, probably because she was a busybody and couldn't keep her nose out of other people's business." He clenched both fists, then quickly opened the injured one and shook it out.

And Gia had to wonder what business of Ben's Gladys had gotten into, because there was definitely anger there. And it seemed personal. "Thanks, Ben. I appreciate the sound advice. I will definitely leave it up to Hunt to figure out who killed Gladys."

"Good." Some of his tension seemed to ease. "Now, would you like a beer or something? It's a nice night to light up the fire pit and sit for a spell."

Or a good excuse to get her into the backyard, surrounded by woods, where there would be no witnesses. "Thanks, Ben. But I have company tonight. Maybe I could take a rain check?"

"You got it. You stop over any time."

"Have a good night, Ben." Gia hurried back across the street, debating whether Ben's advice was just neighborly concern or a warning for her to back off.

Chapter Ten

After calling Hunt to tell him about Ben's bloody hammer and apparently injured hand, and having him assure her he'd look into it, Gia had shoved all thoughts of murder aside. She, Savannah, and Alfie had spent a wonderful evening stuffing themselves full of lasagna, indulging in a huge bowl of rosemary Parmesan popcorn, and binging a few episodes of a seventies' sitcom. All in all, the perfect evening. And, since they'd watched so late, Savannah and Alfie had both spent the night.

When Gia arose, long before the crack of dawn, to get ready for work, she had a renewed pep in her step. Instead of dragging herself out of bed half exhausted, she jumped up and straight into the shower ready to face the day. By the time she'd fed and walked Thor, with a quick glance at the monitors to be sure nothing—human or otherwise—was crouching in wait before she took Thor outside, Savannah and Alfie were up and dressed.

"You want me to make coffee?" Savannah stood beside the counter, coffeepot in hand.

"Nah, if it's okay with you guys, I want to get into the café early." Gia grabbed a tote bag and opened the refrigerator, then took out the container of leftover short rib hash and put it inside the bag. "I want you guys to taste this new hash recipe I'm playing with, and then I have another I want to try out this morning."

Savannah turned a little pale. "After everything I scarfed down last night, the last thing I want to think about this morning is food."

Gia couldn't blame her. "Don't worry, by the time I get around to making this, it'll be well past lunchtime."

Alfie slung his laptop bag cross-body and grabbed Thor's leash. "Come on, big fella, you get to ride in the back with me."

Gia grabbed her purse and keys. "Are you going to ride in with us this morning?"

He hesitated. "That's okay, isn't it? Since I hit my deadline, I have a little spare time before I have to start my next project, and I thought I'd come hang out with you guys for a while."

"Sure." It was always fun having Alfie around. "It's no problem at all. You can always come back for your car whenever."

He beamed at her. "Awesome. Because I have a few ideas."

"Uh-oh. Why do I feel like that should concern me?"

"Don't worry about it. I'm not planning to do anything illegal."

"Whew." She swiped a hand across her brow.

"Yet." He shot her a mischievous grin and bolted with Thor before she could argue with him.

She couldn't help but smile. He was like a rambunctious toddler, too smart and with way too much energy for his own good. "You ready, Savannah?"

"Huh?" Her overnight bag was on the counter, and she looked up from rummaging through it.

"Are you ready to go?"

"Oh, right, yeah. Just give me a minute, I'll lock up behind me and meet you in the car."

"Sure thing." Gia headed for the car with her bags, then stowed them in the trunk. After she slammed the trunk closed, she turned and leaned against it, then took a deep, cleansing breath. It must have rained sometime during the night, because droplets still clung to the leaves and covered the grass.

The sounds of the night still permeated the forest. Insects chirped, birds called to one another, and something large moved through the brush far enough away that it didn't evoke fear. Even before sunrise, the heat and humidity the day would bring had already gripped the forest. The scent of pine filled her, along with the sweet aroma of some flower or another she couldn't identify and the underlying swampy odor of rotting vegetation. No wonder Savannah had loved it out here so much when she'd first found Gia's house.

Of course, the price didn't hurt either. For what she'd have paid for four or five years' rent in New York, she owned an acre of land and a beautiful Spanish-style ranch in what was undoubtedly the most beautiful place she'd ever seen.

Until it had been marred by murder. Although it didn't diminish the beauty, it did put a damper on her enjoyment of it. She considered the porch where she'd seen Gladys and Irene argue. Despite Gia being up and ready to begin her day, most Rolling Pines residents would still be in bed for at least a few more hours. The night had yet to be interrupted by the shouts of children, car doors slamming, the low rattle of garbage pails being rolled to the road. A time of day when no prying eyes should be around to witness anything.

With that thought in mind, she glanced over her shoulder to see if Savannah was coming. She wasn't yet. Before she could change her mind, Gia grabbed a flashlight from the center console, jogged across the street as stealthily as possible and made a beeline for the porch table where Gladys had tossed the notepad. Once she was safely up the steps and sort of concealed behind one of the hedges the HOA had apparently insisted Miley trim, she risked turning on her flashlight. She played the beam over the round side table. The empty tabletop brought a pang of disappointment. Maybe the police techs had already found and confiscated the pad. She slid the light lower.

A red, black, and yellow snake was startled from where it had curled beneath a flower pot, and it lifted its head and stared straight at her.

Gia jerked back, only refraining from screaming because she was too busy hyperventilating. "R-r-red, b-b-b-black, y-yellow, b-bla-black."

The rhyme. How did it go? Savannah had taught it to her when she'd first moved in. Something about red and black to tell the difference between the venomous coral snake and whatever the non-venomous one was called. Red on yellow, kills a fellow. Red on black, friend to Jack. And Gia. Or something like that. It didn't matter, as long as she knew the snake she'd come face-to-face with wouldn't kill her. Nor would Hunt when he found out where she'd come into contact with the critter.

Thankfully, while she stood frozen in panic, the snake slithered off the porch and into the bushes. Now what? She was going to have to pass through those bushes to get off the porch. She could call in reinforcements, if she'd brought her phone with her, which she hadn't. Unfortunately, it was in her purse on the front seat of the car.

She sucked in a deep breath, then another. Her hands shook, flickering the light as she skimmed it along the pavers behind and then under the table with one eye still on the bushes. When the pool of light illuminated something, she jumped before realizing she'd found what she was searching for. "B-bingo."

The notepad must have slid off when Gladys had tossed it onto the table, or sometime when the crime techs were conducting their search. Either way, she was now faced with a dilemma. On the one hand, should she chance removing it from the crime scene when it might contain important information? On the other hand, the techs had already scoured the house and grounds, so if they thought it was important, they'd have picked it up. Right? Of course, they had yet to find the footage Alfie had. Probably. Presumably, the police department would have people poring over that footage. Then again, this surely wasn't their only case.

The silence, and Gia's indecision, were interrupted by Savannah slamming the front door shut.

It was now or never. No way was she leaving empty-handed after that encounter.

"In for a penny, or whatever . . ." she muttered, grabbed the notepad, and hightailed it back across the street, high-stepping to avoid any other snakes that might be slithering around. As she climbed into the car, a moment of panic gripped her. What if Miley's doorbell camera was still running? And certainly, her own cameras had picked up her faux pas. Ugh. When was she going to learn to think before acting and not after?

"Where'd you go?" Savannah frowned at her.

"Trust me, you don't want to know." Gia held up the notepad. "You can't be charged as an accessory if you don't know where this came from."

Savannah laughed and clasped her hands together. "I taught you well, my friend."

"Ha ha."

"Hey, let me savor my proud mommy moment here."

Gia laughed and shook her head as she started the car and backed out of the driveway. She'd do well to remember that Savannah was the far more adventurous of the two of them. But she didn't have to worry about landing in jail, since her husband and cousin were both on the police force. Gia not only had to worry about getting arrested, but about her fiancé finally coming to his senses and calling off the wedding. Huh. Maybe she should take Savannah's advice and get married as quickly as possible. It wasn't like she and Hunt hadn't discussed it. They had. Extensively. Neither of them wanted a big wedding, and they'd already decided to let Savannah and Trevor do most of the planning. So what was she waiting for? "How would you feel about a small wedding on the beach or something?"

Savannah's eyes lit with joy. "For real? You're finally going to plan this?"

"Nope." She shot her a conspiratorial grin. "I'm going to leave it to you and Trevor to plan."

"Yes!" She pumped her fist and bounced on the seat. "Woo-hoo! I'll call Trevor as soon as we get to work."

What had she just done? "Savannah . . ."

She glared pointedly at Gia. "Before you get cold feet and back out."

"Don't you think maybe you should at least wait until the sun comes up to bother Trevor?"

She snorted. "Not a chance, girlfriend."

The remainder of the ride to the café was filled with chatter, mostly Savannah's, about the upcoming nuptials, making Gia slightly queasy. Not that she didn't want to marry Hunt, she did. After her first marriage had failed so spectacularly, she'd never expected to fall in love again. Then, after meeting Hunt, she realized she'd never truly known what it was to love someone so much. Her ex had been a selfish liar and an excellent con man. And she'd fallen for his lies hook, line, and sinker. But their entire marriage had been about him, about his needs, about furthering his career.

Hunt was different. He was kind, caring, and always put others first. He was protective of those he loved, especially Savannah, who he adored. And he loved Gia in a way she'd never been loved before. Even when they did disagree, he always respected her opinions and feelings. And he was patient. He hadn't pushed her once on the wedding date, even though he'd made his position very clear, the sooner the better. Still, no matter how he felt, he'd given Gia the space she seemed to need to overcome her past fears, even warding off Savannah's constant strongly worded suggestions to move forward. And more often than not, when he really did get angry with her, it was out of concern.

"Gia! Hey."

She jerked her foot off the accelerator and let the car slow, searching for anything she might have missed when she'd zoned out. "What?"

"Have you heard a word I've said?" Savannah demanded, her tone more amused than angry.

"Um. Yes?" Satisfied she wasn't about to run anything over, she resumed her drive, careful to pay better attention this time.

"Right. Well, let me just repeat it in case Alfie wasn't listening."

"I heard every word," Alfie piped up from the backseat. "You said maybe, instead of a beach wedding, you could use the beach entry pool at Trevor's mansion."

Thor barked once, possibly in agreement, since he loved Trevor's mansion. And, considering the potty pavilion and doggie playground, why wouldn't he?

Savannah lifted a brow at Gia. "Glad someone was paying attention."

"I'm sorry, Savannah. I was just lost in thought."

She sighed. "Please, tell me it wasn't thoughts of murder."

"No." She smiled at Savannah. "Actually, I was thinking about Hunt, and how perfect my life is now, and how I have you to thank for it all."

Savannah tilted her head and weaved her fingers with Gia's. "Okay, then, I guess I can forgive you for zoning out to think about how wonderful I am."

Gia laughed, and it felt good, eased any lingering concerns or reservations she might have about getting married again. "I don't know how I can ever thank you for everything you've done for me. Setting up the café while I was going through that horrible trial, finding the perfect home for me, even knowing I needed a pet when I didn't know it myself."

Savannah held up a finger. "And don't forget introducing you to my amazing cousin."

"Right, and that." Though she'd actually met him when she'd been his main suspect in her ex-husband's murder investigation, but why split hairs?

"And don't worry about it." She shot Gia her cockiest grin. "I know exactly how you can repay me."

"Oh?"

"Yup, and hold on to all those warm and fuzzy feelings you have going on right now, because it's going to be a doozy."

"Oh, boy." But it didn't matter what Savannah wanted from her, because there was literally nothing Gia wouldn't do for her.

She pulled against the curb in front of the café. While she did occasionally use the back lot, the recently dredged up memories of Bradley's murder had her opting to avoid the lot where he'd been found.

When Alfie offered to walk Thor down to daycare, Gia thanked him and hugged Thor, then left the door open behind her so Alfie would be able to get in. She gestured toward a small table by the front window. "If you want, you can set Alfie's bag down there. I'm sure he's going to want to get started researching something right away."

Savannah scanned the table then looked toward the back room. "Actually, do you mind if I set him up on the island in the kitchen?"

"No, that's fine. Why?" It didn't matter to Gia, and she was pretty sure it wouldn't matter to Alfie, especially since the kitchen was more private, and you never knew what Alfie might try to do. But she was curious as to Savannah's reasons.

"Because now that I'm up and around and excited about getting Trevor down here to plan your wedding, I'm starved. And that new hash you were talking about sounds amazing."

Gia shrugged. Now that she thought about it, she was kind of hungry herself. "I could eat."

"I can get the dining room ready, stock the pastry platters, and start the coffee while you start cooking." Savannah worked her way through the dining room at warp speed, flipping on lights, checking cases, and opening the register. "And, if Alfie's back there with you, he'll be able to keep you updated in real time. I'll come back as soon as the front's ready to open."

"Works for me." Leaving Savannah to see to her chores, Gia brought her tote to the kitchen and slid the short rib hash into the fridge. She pulled out poblano peppers and yellow onions and set them on the island counter.

Savannah stopped in for a minute to set up Alfie's laptop on the counter across from Gia, then pulled one of the stools over for him to sit.

"You want your eggs scrambled, fried, or over easy?" Gia tossed over her shoulder.

"Whatever you're making is fine."

"Okay." She thought about it for a minute, trying to imagine what would go best with the new hash. "I'll just do up a platter of fried eggs, if it doesn't matter."

"Yup. That works." And she disappeared back through the door.

Alfie walked into the kitchen and popped onto the stool, then swung it back and forth. "Thor's at daycare, and Zoe says hi."

"Thank you." As she started the grill, she caught Alfie's rocking in her peripheral vision. "Quit that, Alfie, you're making me motion sick. Don't you ever stay still?"

He seemed to seriously contemplate that for a moment before giving her a cheerful, "Nope."

"You didn't have any trouble with Thor?"

"Not at all. And a word of warning . . ."

Gia grabbed a knife from the rack and turned to look at him. "About?"

"Trevor was already there dropping off Brandy, so he could meet up here with Savannah to start working on wedding plans."

"Ah, man." But that was okay. It was time to stop procrastinating. She loved Hunt and had every intention of spending the rest of her life with him. As long as she was surrounded by the people she loved, the friends she'd become close to since moving to Boggy Creek, the how, where, and when didn't matter. And, as long as she and Savannah were both happy, it wouldn't matter to Hunt either. Now if she could just find a minute when his mind wasn't on murder so she could let him know.

But she grabbed a few more bags of peppers, an extra bag of onions, and a large bag of potatoes. If she made too much, they could always put it on the menu as a limited-time-only special. That would be a good way to gauge customer interest, as well.

"What do you want first, the property records or the notepad?" Apparently, Alfie was ready to get down to business.

"Definitely the notepad." She already knew Gladys owned property in Rolling Pines, so she was more curious about the note she'd scribbled to Irene. Besides, she'd braved a killer snake for that information. Or, at least, what could have been a killer snake.

"You got it." He dug through his bag. "You don't by chance have a pencil, do you?"

"Do you seriously mean to tell me with all that tech you carry around with you, you don't have a pencil?" Gia started peeling potatoes.

"I have pens, but no pencils."

She laughed. "In the middle drawer of my desk."

"Thanks." He took off and returned a minute later, then set the notepad on the counter beside his laptop. "Here goes nothing."

The *scratch, scratch, scratch* as he scribbled over the indentation left in the pad piqued Gia's interest and tweaked her nerves as she started washing peppers and onions, then set them out in stainless steel bowls on the counter. Then, she washed the potatoes and piled them on the counter as well.

Gia hummed softly as she shredded potatoes. Creating new recipes relaxed her, allowed her to recharge and regain her focus. Once she'd finished shredding the entire bag, she set them aside in exchange for the other vegetables.

"Hm."

"What is it?" She paused for a second and glanced over, wary of the fact she was using a very sharp knife.

He frowned, tapped a finger against his chin. "I can't say for sure, but it looks to me like a routing number and an account number."

Why would Gladys give Irene her banking information? Maybe to get the HOA fees? "Like for a bank?"

"Yup." He pounded away on his keyboard for a few minutes while Gia finely diced peppers and onions, the scent beginning to elicit even more hunger. "I was right. The first set of numbers is a bank routing number. Easy enough to find with a simple Google search."

Easy for him, maybe. Gia's results with technology were usually less than stellar. "And the second?"

"I'm assuming the account number, but I'll let you know in a minute."

The implication slammed through her and almost had the knife slipping. She set it aside to stare him down. "Alfie, you aren't seriously considering hacking that account, are you?"

"Of course not, silly." His eyes sparkled with mischief. "I'm already in."

Chapter Eleven

Alfie let out a low whistle.

Despite her worry about him getting into trouble, Gia's curiosity won out. "What did you find?"

"It seems Gladys Hoffmeier wasn't only well-off. The woman was loaded." He turned the laptop so she could see the screen. "I mean, not Trevor wealthy, but no slouch either."

That wasn't saying much considering Trevor's staggering wealth, which she still couldn't wrap her head around sometimes.

"And she definitely didn't need to be mooching off her sister."

"*Half* sister," they corrected together.

"Did you look at the deposits?" Gia asked.

"Not really, just skimmed the total."

Gia finished up dicing the vegetables, filling the stainless-steel bowls, then setting them aside.

Alfie continued to scan and scribble notes.

With the vegetables ready, she added a liberal splash of avocado oil to the already heated grill, then emptied a few packages of chorizo onto one of the puddles, changed her gloves and grabbed a spatula to start breaking it up and spreading it out so it would heat evenly. While that cooked, she poured out the bowls of poblano peppers and onions onto a separate area of the grill.

"Okay, so . . ." Alfie sprang from his stool, reading from the notepad as he spoke. "It seems as if—"

Gia's heart skipped a beat. "Alfie, please, tell me you didn't use Gladys's notepad to take notes." Because they sure did look awfully similar.

"What?" He paused mid-step. "Don't worry about it. I pulled off the top page first."

"But we're going to have to give that to Hunt as evidence." Great, she hadn't even made it down the aisle yet and she was already on the road to divorce.

He swallowed hard. "That probably wouldn't be a good idea, Gia."

"I'm not going to tell him you hacked the account, I'm sure he has someone at the station who can figure that out for themselves.

But I have to give him the notepad." Not only was it the right thing to do, but somewhere along the line someone was going to review the doorbell footage and see Gia taking it. It would be so much better for her if she fessed up beforehand.

"Okay. All right. It'll be fine." Alfie flipped through the top few pages then ripped them off. He set the pad on the counter and stuck the page with the account numbers back on top of it. "There. No harm, no foul."

Gia swiped her brow with her forearm. It would have to be good enough. She returned to turning chorizo and the pepper and onion mixture, careful not to let anything burn as she stirred, keeping an even layer on the grill. The savory yet spicy scent filled the room.

"Do you still want to hear what I found?"

As if she'd say no. "Sure. Go ahead."

"Okay, so." He tapped the pencil eraser against the counter as he spoke. "It seems regular deposits were being made into the account, some through PayPal or Zelle, others as cash."

Why would people be sending Gladys money? Had she come up with some sort of side hustle? They seemed popular enough these days. "Can you trace the deposits back to whoever sent them?"

"Not the cash ones," Alfie answered distractedly, "but the others I can. And two names ring a bell."

"Oh, yeah?"

Tap, tap, tap. Pause. *Tap, tap, tap.* "It probably won't surprise you to know the first is Scott Hoffmeier."

"Not really, considering he told Miley much of the money Gladys left her belonged to him. But why would he send her regular payments? Alimony? Because if the court ordered him to pay alimony, I can't see how he'd think he was entitled to get it back." Then again, Miley had told him as much. But what else had she said? Something about paying for services? Even if Gladys did have some sort of side hustle going, would she really be doing business with her ex?

Alfie frowned and scratched his head. "I don't think it's alimony, though I suppose in Scott's case it could be. But why would the others be sending her regular payments?"

Gia ran several scenarios through her mind. "It could be some kind of passive income source. Or maybe she's selling everything

Scott ever gave her online?" That could be why he felt entitled to the money.

Alfie shook his head. "I don't think so, considering the amounts and frequency are the same for each deposit. Even the cash ones I can't trace are still the same amount, right around the same day of each month."

"Like some sort of subscription service?"

"I guess." Alfie shrugged and lifted his gaze to meet Gia's. "If you subscribe to blackmail."

"Seriously?" Though it wouldn't really surprise her.

"It makes sense. And . . ." He held up a finger. "Not only do I think she was blackmailing people, I think you were her next target."

"Me?" she squealed. Now, that did come as a surprise.

"Yup. She started in with you, kept escalating the situation, and then threatened Thor. I suspect, given what I have to work with so far, that she was about to hit you up for a regular stipend to keep her from pushing the issue. I mean, let's face it, if you weren't engaged to the police captain, she'd have had you once you poked her."

She couldn't deny the truth in his statement. Hunt knew her, understood that Gladys was harassing her. But what if the police captain, or the detectives who showed up when Gladys called, were strangers? What if they believed Gladys's claims that Gia had assaulted her?

Alfie's mouth firmed into a thin line as he studied the information he had on-screen and continued the rhythmic tapping. "I think her end goal was still to get you to pay up; she just had to tread a little more carefully with you. What do you think?"

She wasn't sure what to think, because what Alfie was saying made sense. "If you're right, then it's possible someone she was blackmailing got tired of paying and killed her."

"Or she threatened to expose their secret anyway, or tried to up the payment amount. It could have been anything, really. But whatever happened, I think that woman just pushed someone past their breaking point."

Gia needed time to think, but it did make sense. Had Hunt already figured this much out? Possibly, especially if he checked her accounts, which he may have done as a routine part of his investigation even without having the notepad. Her hopes soared. Maybe they wouldn't have to mention it after all. "You said there were two names I'd recognize. Who was the second one?"

"Want to guess?" He grinned.

It took her less than a second to come up with, "Ben Stettler."

Alfie frowned and shook his head. "Nope. Irene Kellerman."

"Irene?" Her stomach sank.

"Irene's first payment hit the bank a few hours before Gladys was killed."

"Okay. I need some time to think." Because he'd given her an awful lot to digest.

"Take all you need. I'm going to get started on a search of property records." He shifted a few things around, stuffed the notepad into his bag.

Gia piled the shredded potatoes onto the grill with the peppers and onions and began to stir. Though the scent no longer enticed. Instead, it turned her stomach a bit queasy.

The recurrent scraping of the spatula against the grill helped her to focus as she fell into a rhythmic scrape, scrape, turn. No doubt she had to get ahold of Hunt and tell him what they'd found. At least, about the seeming argument between Gladys and Irene and the notepad she'd snatched from the crime scene. She really hoped Savannah and Trevor didn't have their hearts set on a wedding any time soon. If so, they were doomed to disappointment. As soon as Hunt found out the truth.

Once the potatoes were cooked, she began to mix in the browned chorizo.

"Something smells amazing." Cole pushed through the swinging door. "My mouth is watering."

The compliment pleased her, especially since Cole would without a doubt criticize if he thought it was warranted. "Thank you."

He washed his hands and grabbed a fork. "Do you mind?"

"Be my guest." She gave one last stir then went to the fridge for eggs, keeping an eye on him in anticipation of his reaction.

He took a bite, chewed slowly as he savored, then swallowed and turned to her. "You outdid yourself this time, dear. This is amazing."

"I'm thinking of serving it with a roasted poblano salsa."

"Perfect." Cole set his fork in the sink and donned gloves. "You know, you can add this to the dinner menu as well. Not only can you serve it with eggs for a nice breakfast, but you could do it as quesadillas with a side of fresh guacamole as well. The mix is easy enough to prepare and keep. So, what do you want me to do?"

"Do we have avocados?"

"Yup. Delivered yesterday."

"You want to make up a bowl of guacamole, and we'll give it a try?"

"Sounds like a plan." He checked the clock. "You might want to get Earl's breakfast started as well. He should be here soon."

"I'll take care of it." While Earl had given in and tried her home fries, which he ended up loving and adding to his daily routine, he wasn't the most adventurous eater. He'd certainly try a new menu item, and might even eat it for dinner down the line if he liked it, but breakfast was breakfast, and he didn't often stray from his usual. "Oh, hey, Cole, if you want to try the short rib hash, it's in the fridge."

"You betcha." He took out the container, spooned a small helping onto a corner of the grill to heat, then held up the container toward Alfie. "You want to try some of this?"

He looked up from whatever he was doing. "Huh?"

"Gia made short rib and sweet potato hash. What do you say? Want to be a guinea pig?"

"Sure. Why not?" he answered distractedly, then frowned and leaned closer to the screen, muttering to himself.

Cole scooped another spoonful onto the grill.

Gia set sausage and bacon along the back of the grill, then started scooping chorizo hash onto plates and lining them along the counter she used for prep. When she had enough plates for her, Savannah, Alfie, Cole, and Trevor, who should already be there and was probably huddling with Savannah over wedding plans, with a small side dish for Earl, she scooped the remainder into a stainless-steel bin, covered it with plastic wrap, and put it in the fridge.

"You want to add that to the menu this morning?" Cole asked as he popped bread into the line of toasters.

"Yeah, I'll add it to the chalkboard before we open."

"Breakfast or dinner?" he asked.

She shrugged. "I'll start with breakfast and see if there's any left over."

"Okay, then I'll hold off on making the guacamole so it'll be fresh if you want it later."

"Sounds good."

"This doesn't make any sense," Alfie muttered, more to himself than anything.

"What doesn't?" Gia scraped the grease from the chorizo into the grease pan, then sprayed a section of grill with avocado oil and started cracking eggs onto it.

"Take a look at this." Alfie stood and brought his laptop to where they stood at the grill.

Gia kept one eye on the eggs while she glanced at what he pointed out. It seemed to be a map of Rolling Pines but overlayed with colorful splotches. "What am I looking at?"

Cole somehow managed to turn the short rib hash, butter the first batch of toast that popped up, and look over Alfie's shoulder all at the same time.

"Okay, so . . ." Alfie traced a finger along a line up the screen. "This is the road that leads into the development."

She followed his finger when he shifted ninety degrees to the right and continued.

"This is your road." He tapped a spot on the screen. "And this is your house."

"Okay."

"Are you situated?"

She located the HOA office at the front of the development and Miley's and Ben's houses across the street, then Savannah's two blocks over—well, streets, really. She'd yet to get used to the fact that Rolling Pines wasn't set up in a grid pattern like she was used to from New York. The roads curved, dead-ended abruptly, and changed names for no apparent reason. "Okay, I know where you're at. Just give me a minute to take care of these eggs."

He waited, tapping his foot impatiently, while she used a long spatula to flip eggs three at a time down the line, then take them off the grill and slide them on top of the hash.

Probably to keep him from climbing the walls, Cole held out a small plate with short rib hash.

Alfie set his laptop on the counter, took the plate, and dug in with gusto, then sighed. "Oh, mmm, this is amazing. I love it."

Heat crept into Gia's cheeks. While she'd worked the breakfast shift at a busy New York deli for years, that had been more assembly-line cooking—crank the food out as fast as possible so customers could be on their way, many of them biting into sandwiches on their way out the door. Now, she enjoyed being creative, coming up with new ideas, taking her time to see people enjoy what she'd made. And she had Cole to thank for teaching her to slow down and enjoy what she created. She kissed his cheek.

His face flamed red. "What's that for?"

"For teaching me how fun it can be to go out on a limb, be creative, and try new things without fear of criticism." Because when she'd first come to Florida, she'd been a nervous wreck. Bradley had insisted on having things a certain way in his home, and she didn't usually deviate. It had taken her time to move past the anxiety trying something new sometimes brought.

"Oh, well." Holding his plate in one hand, he balanced his fork across it and gave her a one-armed squeeze. "In that case, you're welcome. And, by the way, Alfie's right, this hash is amazing."

Gia grinned, set the spatula aside, and removed her gloves. "Okay, Alfie, show me."

He choked down the rest of his hash, set the dish in the sink and grabbed a napkin to wipe his mouth. Then he returned to the island, cradled the laptop in one arm while she and Cole crowded on either side of him, and picked up where he left off. "Okay. So, these colors represent the flood map. See how your land is high and dry—there's no color over it—and Savannah's is mostly dry except for this small corner of green in the back?"

"Yeah."

"Okay, so this is the property Gladys bought." He tapped a green splotch on the screen. "Which she paid cash for, I might add."

"Seriously?" She tried to remember what lots were going for in Rolling Pines. Last she'd heard, around fifty grand. Where had Gladys come up with that kind of cash? Could be blackmail was more lucrative than Gia realized.

"Yup." He traced a line up to the very top of the development. "She closed on it less than a week ago."

"Why is it all covered in green?"

"Exactly!" He set the laptop aside on the island, apparently having made his point. "A good number of the lots in Rolling Pines have some section of the land in a flood zone. But that entire piece is a flood zone. Whenever we get heavy rains, that piece of property is basically swampland."

"Is it even buildable?" Because what else would Gladys use it for?

Cole started shifting the filled plates to the cutout. "You could build on it, but it would take a lot of time and money to truck in dirt to build the land up. Which seems pointless when the two adjacent lots and one across the street are all relatively dry. And they are all for sale. Granted, that one was the least expensive, but for good reason."

"If it's useless, why is it even up for sale?"

"It's not useless, just not buildable without more effort that it would be worth. As for why it's for sale . . ." Cole shrugged. "Could be any reason. Oftentimes, developers will buy land like that for conservation. Residents will buy up cheap land to preserve natural beauty and keep too many houses from being built in the development. As more people build, and the development becomes more crowded, even swampy land will begin to sell."

"Do you think she got duped?" Wasn't selling swampland in Florida the punch line of more than one joke?

"No way to know." Cole started for the dining room, held the door open for her and Alfie. "Did she strike you as the type to make a major purchase without doing her due diligence?"

"No. Absolutely not." Not that Gia knew her very well, but she seemed too scheming, too conniving, to be taken advantage of. Now, if it had been the other way around, and Gladys had sold the land, she'd have said yes. "So what did Gladys want with a piece of property that was basically useless to her, if her intention was to build a home?"

"I couldn't tell you." Alfie scratched his head. "But isn't that the million-dollar question?"

Chapter Twelve

By the time Gia entered the dining room with Cole and Alfie, Savannah already had the plates on the table and mugs set out, and everyone gathered to eat. Since she was already setting up a tray with coffeepots, creamer, and sugar, Gia headed for the table to eat before they'd have to open.

Earl opened his arms to her, and she went to him for a hug. "Congratulations. I hear wedding bells are ringing."

Yikes! Hunt had better get through this investigation quickly so she could let him know or he'd be hearing about his own wedding through the Boggy Creek rumor mill. Butterflies danced in her belly. "Seems like."

"Well, I think that's wonderful. You're going to make a stunning bride."

Heat flared in her cheeks. "Thank you, Earl."

"Come on. Sit so you'll have time to enjoy your meal instead of having to shovel it down." He gestured toward the table, then went to help Savannah.

"It smells delicious." Trevor stood and pulled out the chair next to him for Gia to sit.

"Thank you, Trevor." She sat, then waited for him to do the same.

First, he leaned close to her ear. "Don't worry, Gia, I've got you covered. And believe it or not, Hunt and I have already discussed some ideas."

Warmth spread through her. Hunt might be patient, but apparently even he wouldn't wait forever.

"Savannah grew up here and she knows, well, pretty much everyone," Trevor continued. "But you are not as outgoing. I promise I won't let Savannah go overboard, no more than a few hundred guests."

"A few hu . . ." She felt every ounce of color drain from her face.

Trevor laughed, deep and contagious, at least under most circumstances.

When faced with the possibility of hundreds of wedding guests staring at her, not so much.

He wrapped an arm around her neck from behind and dropped a

kiss on top of her head. "I'm just messin' with ya. It will be a beautiful but small ceremony, something comfortable for you and Hunt, more suited to your less rambunctious style. Only close friends and family. I promise."

She gripped his hand and leaned into the hug for just a moment. "Thank you, Trevor. For everything."

"You are very welcome. Thank you for trusting me with this." He stood and returned to his seat, then rubbed his hands together. "Now, let's eat. I'm starved, and this looks incredible."

Breakfast was filled with chitchat about flowers, music, dresses, and food. Not that Gia didn't enjoy the wedding planning, and especially the conversation with friends, but her nerves began to get the better of her. She'd spent most of her life trying not to be noticed, to disappear into the background, to be invisible. Being the center of attention was far outside her comfort zone. She set her fork aside and lifted her coffee mug in shaky hands.

"Okay, enough wedding plans for now." Savannah caught her gaze from across the table, winked, and changed the subject. "I want to hear what Alfie found before we get slammed and end up having to wait."

Alfie finished chewing and washed his bite down with a big swig of orange juice, then explained what he'd found about the flood-prone property Gladys had so recently purchased. When no one could come up with any reason Gladys might have done so, they moved onto her finances and the possibility of blackmail.

"Do you really think she planned to blackmail Gia?" Savannah offered a skeptical frown. "Even knowing she's engaged to the police captain? Because that seems like a really brazen move."

"Could be the prospect gave her more of a thrill," Cole offered.

Savannah scowled down at her plate and pushed the food around without taking a bite. "I don't know. It still seems like a foolish choice. If what Alfie found is accurate, the woman had a pretty lucrative side hustle going. Why risk messing it up?"

Gia stared at her food and contemplated returning to wedding plans.

"No one can know that." Alfie stuffed in one last bite of toast, wiped the butter from his fingers, jumped up and ran through the swinging doors to the back room.

Earl scratched his head. "Man, if you could harness that boy's energy, you could power all of Boggy Creek and possibly several surrounding towns."

Trevor watched him go. "Where do you think he's going?"

Gia had no idea, but if she had to guess, he'd come back with some sort of electronic gadget. A smile tugged at her a moment later, though she had to admit to a bit of disappointment that he'd returned with nothing more interesting than his tablet. Although, he piqued her interest when he set the tablet in front of him and pulled out a stylus, then started drawing circles and connecting them with lines.

"Right now, our thoughts are all over the place. There's nothing jumping out at us that connects any of the suspects to Gladys's murder or explains Gia's involvement. So, I figured, let's put together a chart. The visual aid may well show us something we're missing."

Gia sat up straighter, suddenly intrigued. He was right. A scattering of random information made no sense, but somehow, when Alfie organized it all into a coherent form, it sometimes prodded ideas.

"In the center, we have Gladys." He used the stylus to scribble her name in the middle circle, then started filling in the other circles around it. "As far as suspects, Carter Marx has to go on the list, even if Hunt did let him go after questioning him. Just because they didn't have enough evidence to hold him doesn't make him innocent."

"And," Gia added, "I did see him running from the crime scene, he had some sort of run-in with Gladys when he was walking his dog, and he was squatting on the property she bought—which is against the Rolling Pines Rules of Conduct."

"Maybe she was blackmailing him, threatening to turn him in if he didn't pay her," Trevor offered.

Earl shook his head. "Where would he get the money? If he's squatting on land in what basically amounts to a swamp, he probably doesn't have much."

Alfie chewed on the inside of his cheek while he contemplated his chart. The he jotted *property* on the line between Carter and Gladys's names. "Okay, so who else?"

The information Miley Davis had imparted returned front and center to Gia's mind. "Scott Hoffmeier. I overheard him trying to coerce Miley into handing over at least part of the inheritance."

"Good. That's good. Plus, the victim's own sister outright accused him of murdering her." Alfie waved the stylus like he was conducting an orchestra. "And we should add Miley's name too, since she'd recently found out Gladys was mooching off her even though she was loaded."

"And if that weren't enough," Trevor chimed in, "Gladys was having an affair with Miley's husband after Miley had been kind enough to take her in."

"Wait, what?" Earl paused with a forkful of scrambled egg and sausage halfway to his mouth.

Trevor took a moment to update him. "If, that is, Katie is to be believed, which I can't see why she'd have any reason to lie about something like that."

Alfie wrote Scott's name in a circle and *money* on the line connecting him to Gladys. Then he added Miley's name and *affair/money* on her line. "Anyone have any other ideas?"

Gia struggled to organize her thoughts. She had a difficult time moving past Carter as the killer, who'd shown outright hostility toward Gladys, if Ben Stettler had correctly gauged their interaction. Then, the image of the bloody hammer she'd already called Hunt about hit her like a blow. She never did hear back from him about whether he'd found a way to get a warrant to search Ben's garage. "As much as it saddens me to say it, because he seems like a really nice guy, Ben Stettler has to be added."

"You're right." Savannah gestured toward the tablet with her fork. "He had the opportunity, since he lives right next door, on the same side the shadow emerged from the night Gladys was killed. Plus, Gia said even then that she'd found it odd he'd been so cooperative and willing to act as a witness to Gladys harassing Gia right after insisting he minds his own business and keeps to himself."

"I did get the impression he was holding something back that day. And the hammer I found in his garage—" She cut herself off mid-sentence, having forgotten Hunt asked her to keep that quiet. "I . . . uh . . ."

"Just spill it, Gia. The café's not open yet, so there's no one to overhear, and anything you say will be kept at his table." Savannah made an X over her heart with one finger.

With a sigh, and knowing she wouldn't be able to keep her mouth shut after she'd already let the cat out of the bag, Gia swore them all to secrecy, got all-around nods of agreement, then updated them about the hammer with the dark stains on the handle and head. She'd have to ask Hunt's forgiveness later. This newfound deal of always being honest with him was more difficult than she'd anticipated. But she would not enter into a marriage with so much as one single lie between them. She'd already been down that road and had no intention of ever taking that path again. She knew all too well how it felt to be lied to, to be kept in the dark, then be caught by surprise when the truth reared its ugly head.

Even as she conveyed Ben's quick excuse about always leaving DNA behind on his projects, something didn't ring true.

Earl pushed his plate back and folded his hands on the table. "And you were alone in the garage with him, at night, up in Rolling Pines, where no traffic even passes by?"

Noting his agitation, Gia chose her words carefully. She loved Earl, loved that he worried about her and Savannah as if they were his own. He'd more or less adopted her since she'd come to Boggy Creek, and she'd never want to do anything to upset him. "I'll be more careful in the future, Earl, but Savannah and Alfie were right across the street and knew I shouldn't be long. They'd have come looking for me if I hadn't returned in a timely manner."

"Before or after he'd bludgeoned you and dumped you in the yard?"

Touché. "How about if we agree none of us will go anywhere near any of the names on this list alone?"

He nodded and pulled his coffee mug in front of him, apparently mollified by the new agreement.

"I'm adding Irene too." Alfie, apparently oblivious to the tense undercurrents, continued as if no one else had spoken.

Irene. Great. The woman Gia had planned to go see as soon as she could free up some time. She stole a quick glance at Earl.

He quirked one bushy gray brow and held her stare.

She caved and sagged a bit. "I'll take someone with me."

"That's a good girl." He grinned.

She simply shook her head. This whole thing of having people worry about her was new to her, and she loved it, mostly. But it also came with a responsibility to those who cared about her. And that was taking some getting used to.

Alfie jotted Irene's name, then tapped the stylus rapid-fire against his temple. "If that interaction on the front porch was any indication, she was none too happy with Gladys. Plus, aside from Miley, and maybe Scott, she's the only one we know of with a clear motive, since she wired a large sum of money we can only assume was a blackmail payment to Gladys's account."

"But why send a first payment if she was going to kill her anyway? Why leave a trail the police, and any other nosy computer techs, are eventually going to follow?" Gia absently took a bite of hash and egg. It was even better than she'd expected. She took a moment to savor the flavors and decided it would work well as a quesadilla with guac.

"Maybe she didn't plan to kill her." Savannah studied the tablet screen over Alfie's shoulder. "Maybe something happened later that made her go back."

"Or maybe that wasn't the first payment. Maybe she'd been paying cash and was running out of funds. From what I could tell, all of Irene's savings had been drained over the past few months." When no one answered, Alfie looked up to find them all staring at him. Twin red patches flared on his cheeks. "What? I was curious."

With no idea what to say to that, Gia glanced at the clock and did a double take. She should have opened five minutes ago. How had she lost track of time like that? She stood but didn't see anyone waiting by the door, and no one had knocked when they were sitting in clear sight of the window. So, it was all probably fine. She went to unlock the front door then grabbed a bus pan from beneath the counter, returned to the table, and started clearing.

Cole excused himself and headed to the kitchen to clean up and prep the grill.

Alfie followed him, mumbling something about hanging around the back for a while to see what else he could find.

Gia didn't dare think about how he might be planning to do that. She was most likely better off not knowing.

Earl set his coffee on the counter in front of his usual stool and started helping Trevor pile plates from the table.

Savannah added the chorizo hash to the day's specials on the chalkboard then set it on the sidewalk out front and disappeared into the back.

As Gia started a fresh pot of coffee, names churned through her mind—Irene, Ben, Carter, Scott, and Miley. She had to consider them all suspects, and yet, could one of them have really killed Gladys? She knew Irene, Ben, and Miley. Not well, but enough to say hello and shoot the breeze for a bit. Could her instincts about people be that off? Had she become too trusting since leaving New York and all of her ex's deceit behind? The thought had ice-cold dread settling in her gut.

Thinking about trust, or lack thereof, had another thought occurring. Hunt had said Gladys had been forbidden to call 911 because she'd called too many times, but when the police arrived she'd change her mind about whatever she'd wanted to complain about. Could that have been some kind of ploy, a scare tactic to make her victims think she was going to rat them out unless they paid up? Because the day Gladys had harassed Gia, Hunt had eventually gone over to speak to her.

Was it possible someone had seen him there and gotten scared? Killed her out of fear that she was speaking with the police? With the memory came another question. Everyone had thought it odd Gladys would have tried to blackmail a police captain's fiancé, but Gladys had gone about it perfectly. She'd provoked Gia into poking her, which could technically be considered assault. And if Gladys's doorbell camera had picked up the interaction, she would have had proof. Then, Hunt had gone over to see Gladys, which also would have been picked up by the doorbell cam, conveniently without sound to record what he'd said to her.

If Gladys had come to Gia in another day or two, threatened to reveal the footage to Hunt's superiors, said she'd tell them Gia had assaulted her and Hunt had refused to arrest her, what would she have done? She wouldn't have been able to prove her innocence, and Gladys would have had solid proof, even if it was a lie. So, how would Gia have handled it? Would she have paid her? A chill ripped through her, raising goose bumps, because she honestly didn't know.

Chapter Thirteen

With Cole working the grill, Savannah waiting tables, and Earl still nursing his coffee at the counter and available for backup if needed, Gia had the luxury of greeting customers and keeping her ears open for any news, a.k.a. good dirt. So far, she hadn't learned anything new. She'd settled in the front corner of the dining room beside the big picture window and spent nearly as much time enjoying Main Street as she did staring at the laptop on the table in front of her.

With a sigh, she shifted her gaze from the beautiful clear blue sky to continue scrolling through social media she rarely used for anything other than advertising. Unless you counted searching for murder suspects. It wasn't her first choice of tasks, but Alfie had assured her it was about the only thing on the list she was technically advanced enough to deal with. Plus, if she remained out front, he argued, it allowed her plausible deniability with Hunt should the need arise.

Whatever that meant he was up to, she had no idea, and she'd just as soon keep it that way. So, she'd simply taken his word for it and settled beside the window with a second cup of coffee—and then a third—before finally switching to herbal tea when she started to feel jittery. Though she had a feeling the jitters came more from the feeling they were finally beginning to make progress than the amount of caffeine she'd ingested.

She'd been searching through Irene Kellerman's social media all morning, scrolling through her Facebook friends list for the past half hour. The woman was a lot more socially active than Gia, and it had taken Gia the past few hours to weed through her Facebook posts for the past six months, figuring that's the longest Gladys could have been blackmailing her, or anyone else in Rolling Pines, since that's when she'd moved in.

Before that, Gia had gone through Irene's Instagram, her TikTok, and the Homeowners Association Facebook page. Irene hadn't posted on any one of them that Gladys had been blackmailing her or that she'd taken revenge by killing her. Wouldn't want to make Gia's job too easy. Actually, Hunt's job, since Gia's job was technically running the café, not investigating a murder. Then again, since when had that stopped her?

With her thoughts scattered all over the place, the name Marx took a moment to register, and she had to scroll back up. "Well, well, well, Irene. What have we here?"

A small twinge of disappointment started to settle in when she realized the account on Irene's friends list didn't belong to Carter Marx, but to a woman named Cindy Marx. Gia clicked on the profile anyway. The first image to pop up was of an attractive older woman, her dark hair streaked with the first bits of gray worn up in a carefree bun. Her smile was wide, her eyes clear and lit with humor, and her expression happy.

Gia scrolled through a few posts, noted nothing of interest other than the fact that she shared a surname, and a fairly common one at that, with one of their suspects. That, and the fact that despite their seemingly polar opposite character and age difference, the resemblance between Cindy and Carter was remarkable.

Though Cindy made no reference to Carter at any point throughout ten years of Facebook history, nor did any of the hundreds of photos Gia waded through show the two of them together, Gia had no doubt they were somehow related. Was she Carter's mother? His aunt? Although she didn't appear old enough, Gia supposed she could be his grandmother, but it didn't seem likely.

Since there were no mentions of other family members, Gia started on Cindy's friends list and jumped straight to the M's to search for anyone else who shared her last name.

"Hey."

Startled, Gia jumped. She hadn't even realized she'd lost herself so completely in the middle of the café. At least they weren't busy, thanks to the lull between breakfast and lunch. "Oh, hey, Alfie. What's up?"

Alfie dropped onto the chair next to hers and set his laptop in front of him. "Find anything interesting?"

"Um . . . I found something. I'm just not quite sure what yet." She gestured to the laptop, assuming he'd brought it with him for a reason. Hopefully, that he'd solved Gladys's murder. "How about you?"

"Nah. I'm at a standstill. Mostly because I can't think of anything else to look for. I was hoping you'd have some ideas."

She turned her screen a bit so he could see it but no one else could. "I found this woman, Cindy Marx, who bears an uncanny resemblance to Carter, but I can't find any connection between them. Carter has no social media that I can find, and Cindy never mentions him, so . . ."

"Here, let me see." Alfie pulled the laptop closer to his own, then set to work.

Gia stood, stretched to ease the stiffness that had begun to settle in her back. She'd sat for too long. She needed to move around. Savannah could probably use a break, anyway, so she'd take over and deal with any new customers who came in and give her a chance to get off her feet.

Gia glanced over at her friend and wondered, not for the first time, how she managed to spend all day on her feet in those arch killers she adored so much. Whenever Gia asked, she simply laughed it off and said it was the price she was willing to pay for fashion.

"Cynthia Marx is Carter's older sister."

Gia turned her attention back to Alfie. "Are you sure?"

"Positive. She's fifteen years older than him, but they are definitely siblings. I found the match on one of those DNA websites."

"You hacked another database," she hissed, mindful of anyone who might be eavesdropping.

"Actually, no. It's a public family tree, and their names and birthdates are both listed on it. Do you want me to dig in further?"

Did she? For what purpose? They couldn't go randomly invading people's personal lives. Wasn't that why police officers needed warrants? "Not right now, but thanks. I'd be more interested to know what her connection to Irene is. If there even is one. You know how social media can be, you end up friends with acquaintances, friends of friends, and even total strangers you've never met, but still . . ."

"Yeah, still." Alfie nodded somberly. "Gladys was killed, and Irene and Carter are both potential suspects in her murder."

"In our minds, anyway," she reminded herself as well as him, because Hunt had said no such thing. Although he had brought Carter in for questioning. "All right, I'm going to relieve Savannah for a bit and think on some of this, could you—"

A tremendous crash interrupted her, and she whirled toward the sound.

Savannah stood frozen amid an overturned bus pan and dishes

scattered and broken on the floor around her. A chair lay on its side amid the mess.

Gia rushed to her side, wrapped an arm around her, and guided her toward a nearby chair, which Alfie turned around for her to sit. "Are you okay? Are you hurt?"

Savannah looked up at her, tears tracking down her cheeks. "I'm so sorry, Gia. I don't know what happened. I turned, and I guess the pan must have caught on the chairback, and it tipped. I tried to catch it, but I couldn't get it rebalanced. I—"

"Hey, Savannah, calm down. I don't care about the dishes." Gia smoothed a few loose strands of hair behind Savannah's ears. "I just want to make sure you're okay."

Savannah sniffed, nodded. "I'm fine. I just have a lot on my mind lately, and I guess I just wasn't paying attention."

"Do you want to talk about what's bothering you?"

"No, no. Like I said, I'm fine." She gave a small chuckle. "I think maybe I just need some normalcy, without murder interfering. I need my husband to come home at night so I can sleep in my own bed. I need a lazy morning where I can sleep in and have breakfast in bed."

Gia could certainly understand how she felt. She'd barely spoken two words to Hunt since Gladys was found, and those had all involved the investigation in one way or another. At the rate they were going, Hunt would be finding out about the wedding on his way down the aisle.

Still, while she wasn't quite sure Savannah was being fully forthcoming, she couldn't push her at the moment. Unfortunately, the incident had caused every pair of eyes in the café to fall on Savannah, and all of the gossipmongers continued to stare, probably waiting for some juicy tidbit they could run off and share.

Gia took a deep breath, reined in her emotions, then let it out slowly. After everything Savannah had been through, Gia had become overprotective. But, surely, most of the onlookers were simply concerned. "You're sure you're not hurt?"

"Positive." She stood and brushed off her hands. "I'm fine."

"Well, I was just coming to take over for you anyway, so you could take a break. Would you like to take the rest of the day off?"

She scowled at Gia. "What would I do with the day off when you're here and Leo's wrapped up in this investigation?"

Gia grinned. "Okay, then, go sit and relax a few minutes. Go in my office if you want. I'll get this cleaned up and take over your tables."

Savannah reached for the bus pan, but Alfie beat her to it. "I can—"

Gia gripped her arm. "Go. Sit."

She huffed out a breath but finally gave in, stepped over the mess, then went behind the counter and grabbed a Diet Coke. She stood for a moment, seemed to think better of the idea, and swapped it for a water.

Alfie was already stacking broken plates in the bus pan. "I'll get this, Gia. You go ahead and take care of the customers."

"You're sure?"

"Positive."

Cole set a broom and dustpan aside and bent to help. "Go ahead, Gia. Alfie and I will clean up."

"All right. Thank you." She spared a glance to be sure Savannah had taken time to recoup and caught sight of her heading to the back with her water and a couple of muffins. Relieved that she was taking a break she clearly needed, Gia grabbed a coffeepot and made a quick round to check for refills.

• • •

By the time the front door opened and Hunt walked in, things were back in order and Savannah had returned. He stopped to kiss Savannah's cheek, then gave Gia a quick hug and dropped onto a stool at the counter.

Gia filled a mug with coffee and set it in front of him, then leaned on the counter to chat. She contemplated letting him know the wedding plans were in the works, then noted how tired he looked. "Can I get you something to eat?"

"Yes, please. I don't even care what it is, but I'm starved and I might have to run out at any moment." Since damp tendrils of dark hair curled over his collar, he must have already taken time for a shower, which meant his meal time was limited. Talk would have to wait for later. It would be better to find a private moment anyway, maybe over a romantic dinner. She popped a blueberry muffin in the toaster behind the counter. "Give me a quick second to ask Cole to make you something."

He nodded and sipped his coffee, then closed his eyes for a moment and tilted his head back and forth.

After asking Cole to make something quick, she plated the muffin, buttered it, and set it on a place mat in front of Hunt. It would have been better on the grill, but at least this way he'd get something in his stomach in case he got called back in.

While there were other customers in the café, none were in the immediate vicinity, and she felt reasonably confident she could speak quietly without being overheard from where she stood behind the counter facing him. "How are things going?"

"I'm okay, just exhausted." Hunt was in tune enough with her to understand she was asking about his well-being as well as the case. "And I don't have anyone in custody yet."

"I heard you brought Carter Marx in for questioning."

A smile played around the corners of his mouth. "You did, huh?"

She shrugged. "The Bailey sisters were in."

That elicited a chuckle. "Of course they were."

"Did you ever find a way to look into that other thing I mentioned?"

"I did, actually. I was at the crime scene and decided to recanvass the area. It just so happened Ben's garage door was open at the time, and he was inside working on a truck."

Her heart rate kicked up. "And?"

"I spotted the item in question on the tool bench, asked him about it, and got pretty much the same answer you did. He laughed it off, but when I asked if I could take the hammer in to be tested, he balked a little. But he eventually consented."

She held her breath.

"The lab tech was able to tell me there were two blood types on the hammer, one of which matched Gladys's blood type, though the DNA results are still pending. But the ME believes *a* hammer was the murder weapon. She hasn't yet confirmed it was *that* hammer." He broke off a piece of muffin, popped it into his mouth.

Her lungs began to ache, and she blew out the breath she'd been holding. "So, what does that all mean?"

"It means I can ask Ben to come in for questioning, but I wouldn't be able to arrest him yet unless he blurted a confession." He finished off the muffin and started on his coffee.

She wasn't sure how to feel about the new circumstances. On the one hand, it would be a relief, especially with how Gladys's murder had affected Savannah so badly, to have the killer apprehended. But, on the other hand, she liked Ben. He seemed like a nice guy, and she'd hate to think her opinion of him could be that far off. Then again, she had no idea what might have pushed him to the breaking point. *If* he was even the killer. "What are you going to do?"

Cole emerged from the kitchen and set a plate filled with chorizo hash, fried eggs, and home fries in front of Hunt. "It was the quickest I could do, since I already had everything out."

"It's perfect, thank you."

Gia set a napkin and fork in front of him, and he dug in.

"You bet." He turned to Gia. "We're running low on western omelet mix, and the peppers and onions won't be delivered until tomorrow. Do you want to take them off the menu for tomorrow morning?"

"No, they sell pretty well." And the last thing she wanted to do was remove something people came in specifically for. "I'll just run to the store after Hunt is done and pick up a few things."

He gave a curt nod. "Good enough. I'll run a quick inventory and see if there's anything else we need."

"Great, thanks, Cole." She waited for him to push back through the swinging doors before repeating her question. "What are you going to do about Ben?"

"Nothing yet. I'm going to investigate, see what the ME and lab techs come up with, and then I'll decide. Hey, this hash is delicious."

"Thank you. There's probably more if you want?"

"No, I'm good, but thanks."

She returned to her line of questioning, knowing a stalling tactic when she saw it, though he did seem to enjoy the hash. "Do you think he did it?"

Hunt took a few more bites before answering. "My gut says no, but I honestly don't know, so do me a favor?"

Hopefully. "Sure, what?"

"Just stay away from him, don't be going over there alone or anything, while I figure this out?"

She nodded. For once he'd asked for a promise she could keep—probably.

Chapter Fourteen

Gia filled a few produce bags with green bell peppers and dropped them into her cart, then she grabbed a couple bags of yellow onions and set them in as well. She'd learned her lesson the hard way not to go into the store without a cart, even if she only meant to buy a few things. Somehow, she always ended up with more than she'd planned to buy. She contemplated the other produce, then picked up a few packages of perfectly ripened strawberries and blueberries.

Of course, she'd need pound cake and whipped cream if she wanted to make dessert, since she wouldn't have time to make them from scratch. She hurried to the necessary aisles, thankful she knew the layout of the store so well. She should probably think about something for dinner, but there was still plenty of leftover lasagna, since Hunt and Leo had never stopped by to eat. If she wasn't mistaken, there should be barbeque left as well.

When her cell phone rang, she dug through her purse, pulled it out, and had a moment of anxiety when Savannah's name showed on the screen. "Hey, Savannah, what's up? Everything okay?"

"Right as rain."

Her insides settled when it seemed Savannah's usual sunny disposition had returned. She should take a day off, ask Cole, Willow, and Skyla to run the café, and surprise Savannah with a spa day. Maybe even follow it up with a trip to the mall.

"But are you still in the store?"

"I am. Why? Do you need anything else while I'm here?" She scooped up a pound cake on her way to the refrigerator aisle.

"Could you pick up some paper towels? We're running low."

"No problem. Anything else?" She added the whipped cream into the cart.

"Nope. That'll do." Savannah hesitated. "Hurry back, though."

"You're sure everything's okay?"

"Yes, but . . . uh . . . the Bailey sisters were just in. They said to say hello and tell you they were sorry they missed you." Clearly, Savannah was making the call amid prying ears.

Gia smiled, easily able to read between the lines with Savannah. "Good dirt?"

"Interesting, at least."

"Can't wait to hear it." She made a beeline for the proper aisle, tossed a package of paper towels into the back of the cart, and headed for the register, her mind racing ten steps ahead of her feet as she tried to imagine whatever gossip Estelle and Esmeralda had managed to unearth.

As she waited on line, she caught a glimpse of the sky from the front window. When she'd walked in fifteen minutes ago, the sun had been shining. Now, dark clouds had begun to gather, casting a shadow across the parking lot. While late-afternoon thunderstorms were a common occurrence in Florida, she didn't feel like getting caught in a downpour then having to spend the rest of the afternoon and evening in the air-conditioned café.

Watching the storm brew, she rocked from foot to foot and willed the line to move faster, then inched forward and caught sight of a familiar figure in the parking lot.

Irene Kellerman hurried across the strip mall parking lot toward her car.

With two people left in front of her on line, Gia would never catch up with Irene if she waited her turn. Instead, she backed out of the line, pushed her cart to the side, and called to the cashier that she'd be right back as she ran past. Thankfully, the sneakers she always wore for work made it easy to catch up to the other woman, who tottered across the lot on four-inch heels.

Gia slowed as she approached, trying to catch her breath. "Irene?"

Irene whirled toward her. A gust of wind rippled a clear plastic dry-cleaning bag, covering only one garment, hung over her arm. "Oh, hello, Gia."

"Hi. How are you?" If Gia wasn't mistaken, the bag contained the same peach suit Irene had been wearing the day she'd visited Gladys—the same day Gladys had been killed.

"I'm doing well, and you?" She scanned the lot as they spoke, her gaze darting from place to place without staying still for more than a second at a time.

"I'm good, thank you." And with that, she ran out of conversation. She'd been so eager to talk to Irene, and now that they were face-to-face, she couldn't remember any of what she'd wanted to ask her.

Irene frowned. "It's such a shame about Gladys, isn't it?"

As far as openings went, Gia couldn't have planned it better herself. "It's so sad. And scary to think whoever killed her hasn't been caught yet."

Her face paled. "I know what you mean. I double-check the locks on my doors about ten times a night before I go to bed. And even then, I barely sleep."

No wonder her complexion was so pallid, and dark circles ringed her eyes. Gia could certainly sympathize with lying awake all night. But fear of the killer wasn't the only thing making Gia lose sleep. "Plus, I can't help feeling guilty that I argued with her the day she was killed."

"Oh, no." Irene gripped Gia's hand. "You can't possibly blame yourself for that."

Gia shrugged. Knowing the argument hadn't been her fault, and that Gladys had been a difficult woman, didn't stop her from replaying their final argument over and over in her mind, searching for a way she could have handled things better. Unfortunately, each replay ended the same way, with her furious over Gladys threatening Thor. But could Gia have deescalated the situation before it had reached that point? She'd never know. And that's probably what kept her up at night. When Irene didn't offer any more—like *I know how you feel*, or *I had an argument with her too*—Gia decided to give her a nudge. "I've heard rumors that others in Rolling Pines had similar problems with her . . ."

She let the question trail off without specifying what the problems might have been. But if Irene wanted to assume she was talking about the blackmail, so be it.

"Yes . . . um . . . Yes, I've heard talk of others having issues. Apparently, Gladys liked to spend her time searching for people's deep, dark secrets and divulging them to the police."

"Oh, really? I hadn't heard that." At least, not exactly that way.

"Well," Irene backtracked. "I'm not sure she ever told the police anything, but she would call them out, certainly scare her victims, then send the officers on their way. I've heard from more than one officer they were told to cuff her and take her into the station if she dialed 911 once more and didn't have a life-threatening emergency to report."

"I did hear that part." About ten times.

Irene glanced up at the roiling clouds then returned her attention to Gia. "Have you heard anything at all about who the police suspect?"

Gia shrugged, tiptoeing through dangerous territory as she balanced what was public knowledge with what Hunt had told her privately, which was very little, and the speculation she and her friends had come up with, which wasn't much more. No sense starting gossip that would ruin anyone's reputation with few to no facts. "I heard they questioned Carter Marx, but as far as I know they let him go. Do you know him?"

Her eyes widened, not a lot, but enough for Gia to catch the reaction. "I, uh . . . I mean, I know who he is."

"Rumor has it, he was squatting in Rolling Pines, but I thought that was against the rules and regulations." Gia frowned, watching Irene closely. If she hadn't been, she'd have missed the way her gaze skipped to the right before returning to Gia. "Were you aware he was living there?"

"Oh, my." She bunched the dry-cleaning bag between her hands, probably wrinkling her newly pressed suit. The wind whipped up, tumbling a palm frond across the lot. "Oh, Gia. Please, don't tell anyone this, but I may need you to speak to Hunt for me."

"Is everything okay?"

"No, no. Not at all." Clutching her suit tightly against her body, Irene huffed a breath. Tears welled in her eyes, shimmered, turned them a darker shade of blue that reminded Gia of deep, turbulent water. "It's just . . . I knew Carter was squatting on the land out there. I have for quite some time. Just like I know Ben Stettler is running an auto shop out of his garage and those sheds in his yard."

Gia's motive radar pinged wildly. At least now she knew the secret she'd been so sure Ben was keeping. The only question remained, was it enough of a motive for him to kill Gladys to keep anyone from finding out? If she'd turned him in, he'd have lost his livelihood. Definitely a major problem, but enough of one to commit murder?

"I'm well aware that as the president of the HOA, it's my responsibility to uphold the rules, and to see that every resident adheres to all regulations, but who were they hurting? Carter keeps to himself, pitching a tent on a useless piece of swampland for him and his dog. He doesn't bother anyone, so what was the harm? And Ben is a nice guy."

Unless he was a killer. Then, not so much.

"He needs that income to pay his mortgage. He has over an acre lot with a small, three-bedroom ranch on it. Why should all that land go to waste while he pays an exorbitant amount of rent for a shop somewhere else? Plus, he's kind enough to give all Rolling Pines residents discounts when they need work done."

"So, what was Gladys's problem with the two of them? Ben said Carter walked by one day and gave her a dirty look."

"Gladys's only problem was that she just could not mind her own business. She was always watching to see what everyone else was doing. And she couldn't stand when someone was getting away with something she didn't have. It didn't matter that she was blessed with a nice home to live in, it still burned her bonnet that Carter was living for free. Even if it was in a swamp."

So was Gladys living for free, from everything Gia had heard. Was that why she'd been freeloading off her sister? Because she was jealous that Carter wasn't paying to live there?

Irene grew more and more upset as she spilled her story. "And, not only did she threaten to turn him in, when the police would no longer take her calls, she went and bought the property he most often squatted on just so she could throw him out. Who does that?"

"I don't know. That's awful." And she meant it, though it still didn't justify murder.

"And don't even get me started on poor Scott. I don't know what it was, but she has been holding something over that man's head since before they were married, even roped him into getting hitched and supporting her." It seemed Irene had been holding all of this in for too long, and everything that was on her mind spewed out of her mouth as if she had no control over it. "And despite his loyalty, and him trying to make the best of a bad situation, she accused him of cheating on her when he was just being kind and offering comfort to a friend."

Gia was beginning to think Irene might have wished things were different. She either had some interest in Scott or really despised Gladys. Who knew? Maybe both. It didn't escape Gia's notice, though, that she didn't share her own interaction with Gladys, that she made no mention of the argument they'd had. And, while she *had* told Gia about the secrets she'd been keeping, they all involved someone else. Had Irene paid the blackmail money to keep Carter from getting thrown out or making Ben shut down his business? Or simply to keep anyone from finding out she knew about the others so she wouldn't get fired? Of course, she could always have denied any knowledge, so that didn't seem right. It seemed there had to be something more there. Perhaps Irene had a secret of her own.

When the wind picked up and the first drops of rain began to fall, she kept on going with her rant. "That woman was ridiculously jealous of everyone, especially Miley, who was kind enough to take her in when she walked out on her husband. And how did she repay her, aside from freeloading? She stole the woman's husband, cheated with him right there in Miley's own yard. Not that I'm putting all the blame on her, mind you. Elijah certainly had a role to play too, but Gladys could also have said no, could have shown some loyalty to her own flesh and blood, even if she had none for her husband."

It was quite clear exactly where Irene felt Gladys's loyalty should have lain.

The hair on Gia's arms stood on end. Lightning forked from cloud to ground, way too close for comfort, followed almost immediately by a peel of thunder loud enough to rattle car windows. If she didn't want to get soaked, it was time to go. Plus, she still had to go back inside for her purchases. Otherwise, she'd have stood there until Irene ran out of steam or dirt, whichever came first.

"Oh, my. I'd better run. I'll speak to you soon, Gia." She looked warily up at the churning dark clouds. "And if you hear anything new, please feel free to stop by the office and let me know."

"I will, and same goes," she called after her.

As Irene hurried across the lot, Gia's gaze once again fell on her nude pumps. Only, this time, she noted muddy stains on the heels. Gia was pretty sure they were the same ones she'd been wearing at Gladys's. Yet, at the time of the doorbell footage, the ground had been bone-dry, so her heels wouldn't have sunk into any mud. It hadn't rained until after her confrontation with Gladys, from what Gia could remember. The hairs on her arms stood up once again, but this time it had nothing to do with an impending lightning strike.

To be fair, the best she could tell from the video was that Gladys had been wearing a peach suit and nude pumps. For all Gia knew, she might own ten of each. She'd have to ask Alfie to pull the video back up, then look at the later footage to see if Gladys had returned later on that night.

Gia jogged back into the store, praying she'd have enough time to pay for her purchases and throw them in the car before the storm unleashed its fury. Thankfully, her cart was exactly where she'd left it, and the lines at the registers had cleared out, probably because everyone was trying to beat the storm.

She jumped on the express line, paid, hooked the bags over her arm, and grabbed the paper towel package. Pretty sure she had everything, she left the cart and headed for her car just as the sky opened up and dumped a torrential downpour.

She splashed to her car, threw her stuff onto the backseat, then jumped inside and wiped the rain from her face. She flipped down the visor to look in the mirror, wiped a bit of black mascara that had begun to run beneath her eyes, and tied her dripping hair up into a sloppy knot. It was the best she could do for now. Thankfully, she'd started leaving clean clothes in the apartment above the café, so she could change into something dry as soon as she got back.

Ever since she'd promised herself she'd never rent it out again, she'd kept the space for herself and Savannah to use when they worked late or had to get up early or just didn't feel like making the twenty-minute drive out to Rolling Pines. Although, come to think of it, they hadn't bothered staying over at all recently. While Gia could easily pick Thor up at daycare and walk upstairs, it would still mean leaving Klondike and Pepper alone. Huh. Maybe it was time she think about renting it out again. She certainly could use the income, and there had to be a decent tenant out there somewhere. Probably. They couldn't all be bad. Right?

She slapped the visor back up, then started the car and turned off the air-conditioning. With her head filled with thoughts of dry clothes and a warm cup of coffee, she started out of the lot. As she turned out onto the road, she spotted Irene parked along the curb.

She stood outside the open driver's door with a pink umbrella, which was doing her very little good against the windswept rain.

Gia pulled over and parked a few cars back, resigned to the fact that she'd have to get back out again to see if the woman needed help.

Before she could reach for the door handle, a dark, hunched figure emerged from the alleyway between two buildings. Whoever it was jumped into Irene's passenger seat and pulled the door shut behind him. Him? Yes. At least, she thought so.

Irene glanced around the empty street and closed her umbrella as she slid into the car.

Figuring she didn't need help after all, and grateful not to have to get back out and get soaked, Gia pulled away from the curb behind her. She crept along, her windshield wipers barely keeping up with the deluge. When they reached the point where Gia had to turn, either to head to the café or the opposite direction toward Rolling Pines, she hesitated. She hit her signal to turn in the direction of the café, reminded herself it was none of her business whom Irene had picked up, then sighed and followed her toward Rolling Pines anyway.

Chapter Fifteen

When the rain let up, Gia hung back. Not that she didn't have reason to head to Rolling Pines, considering she lived there and hadn't mentioned heading back to the café to Irene, but she'd prefer neither Irene nor her passenger catch sight of her. Considering the road that led to their development ran straight through acres and acres of prehistoric forest, she didn't really risk losing them. So, keeping her distance, she kept pace with Irene's car, then slowed when she turned into the development. Most likely, Irene was either heading home or to the office, and Gia wanted to give her time to park. If she could time it right, she'd pass by just as her secret passenger emerged. Then she could just beep and wave, stop home for a few minutes for legitimacy, and head back to the café.

She'd already been gone too long. Plus, Savannah had said the Bailey sisters had dug up good dirt. As she passed the HOA office parking lot, she spotted Irene's car, but there was no sign of anyone getting out. She must have allowed too much time.

Maintaining her speed, she crept slowly past, even watched in her rearview mirror for any hint of movement. Nothing. When she reached her road, she turned and pulled into her driveway.

Rocky, her resident raccoon, sat atop her recycle bin with leftover barbeque from the open bear-proof garbage pail next to him spread before him like a feast. Instead of fleeing when she pulled in, he simply stared at her curiously and continued to chow down. While she didn't want to keep him from eating, she couldn't leave that mess where it was either. There was no telling what might be waiting for her when she got home later, possibly after dark, if she didn't clean up.

She sighed and shoved the door open, got out, stood beside the open door with her hands on her hips and stared him down.

Rocky tilted his head and took another bite.

"Seriously?" Knowing full well who was going to win this battle, Gia contemplated walking down the driveway to get her mail. But what if Rocky got tired of ribs and decided to pounce? What if one of his forest friends, like the black bears that often roamed the neighborhood in search of a meal, stopped by for a visit? Keeping one eye on Rocky, she leaned back into the car and grabbed the bear spray Hunt had given her from her purse. Thankfully, she'd never had to use it, but better safe than sorry. Leaving Rocky to eat his fill, Gia strolled down the driveway to her mailbox, opened it, and looked inside. Empty.

She straightened, contemplated Miley's house. Crime scene tape still stretched across the front, which meant she should probably stay away. But she couldn't get Irene's mud-stained heels out of her mind. Even though it had rained cats and dogs by the market, the storms had yet to reach Rolling Pines. Once they did, though, any sign of heel prints might disappear. Of course, the police had probably already noted and photographed any that might have been in the yard. Still . . .

What could it hurt to have a quick peek? She had to do something while she waited for Rocky to finish eating. She dashed across the street before she had time to come to her senses. Ben was nowhere in sight, and his house was closed up tight, though she couldn't see into the sheds and outbuildings she now knew he used for his business. She skirted the crime scene tape and walked up the side yard bordering Ben's property.

What was she even looking for? The police had already searched the house and property. What could she find that they would have missed? The notepad had been a fluke, since it had fallen behind the table, and they would have had no reason to search there. No doubt they'd return to look for it as soon as someone had time to review all of the doorbell camera footage. Which reminded her, she was going to have to tell Hunt about that and turn over the pad to him. She should have done so already.

She surveyed the yard. While the front lawn was neat and well-manicured, the back was nothing but scattered patches of dirt, grass, and weeds. And a smattering of holes Gladys had accused Thor of digging. She paused beside the row of hedges Gladys's attacker had emerged from. She bent over and peered beneath the bush, leaned to see between the hedges. Nothing stood out. She scanned the lawn where markers showed the spot where Gladys had fallen. When she spotted the small circular puncture marks in the dirt, her chest tightened. She looked around to be sure no one was watching then moved closer to the marks. Since Savannah wore heels all the time, no matter the occasion, she recognized heel impressions in the dirt when she saw them. But what did they mean? Had Irene been in the yard at some point? Had Miley walked back there for some reason, perhaps to pay tribute to her sister? Could Gladys have left them herself? Probably not if she'd been wearing the same chunky heels she'd had on when she'd confronted Gia.

The sun emerged just then from behind a cloud, and Gia shielded her eyes. She should have worn her sunglasses. She started to turn away, needed to go clean up her garbage and get back to the café, especially since tailing Irene and her cohort had proved to be a dead end. And she was dying to know what the Bailey sisters had shared with Savannah.

A glint from among a patch of weeds caught her eye. A trick of the sun? She ducked beneath the crime scene tape and moved closer. She bent down and parted the weeds. The sun reflected off an earring half buried in the mud. She picked it up. A pearl post with no back.

Sweat slicked her hand and she nearly lost her grip on the bear-spray canister. Should she take the earring with her, or put it back where she'd found it and just tell Hunt about it? Of course, if whoever had dropped it came back before he could retrieve it . . .

With no further thought, she cupped the earring in her hand and stood.

The back garage door swung open just then, and a man wearing a camo hoodie emerged and skidded to a stop.

Gia aimed the bear spray and depressed the plunger. At least, she tried to. When nothing happened, her gaze shot to the man.

Even with his hood pulled low, there was no mistaking the shocked expression on Carter's face as he froze, then turned and bolted across the backyard and disappeared into the woods. Had he been the shadow that had overtaken Gladys?

Gia studied the canister, then realized she'd forgotten to flip the safety off, which was probably for the best, considering Carter hadn't posed any threat, had, in fact, run the other way when confronted.

Her first instinct was to call Hunt, but she'd left her cell phone in the car along with everything else. She hurried back across the street, bear spray ready, scanning her surroundings for any sign of Carter.

At least Rocky had eaten his fill and disappeared. Or maybe he'd been scared off by something. She increased her speed, huffing and puffing by the time she reached the car. She should probably think about some kind of consistent exercise routine.

As soon as she reached her car, she jumped inside and locked the door, then breathed a sigh of relief as she fumbled the phone out of her purse and hit Hunt's number.

He answered on the first ring. "Hey, Gia, what's up?"

"I just ran into Carter Marx. He was coming out of Miley's garage, and I would have pepper-sprayed him, but I forgot about the safety, and . . ." She sucked in a deep gulp of air.

"Hold up, Gia. Where are you?"

"Oh, right. I'm sitting in my driveway right now, but I walked across the street while I was waiting for Rocky to finish his lunch, and that's when I ran into Carter."

"Gia, slow down. What are you talking about? Why aren't you at the café?"

Oh, right. She probably should have started with that, but then she'd have to admit to tailing Irene after a man had jumped into her car. Had it been Carter? Had she driven him from town out to Rolling Pines so he could break into Miley's house for some reason? But the police had already combed through the house, what could he have been hoping to find? Then again, she'd found the earring—

"Gia!"

"Oh, sorry, Hunt." Her mind had wandered. "Also, I found an earring by where Gladys was found."

Silence hummed through the speaker.

She tried to wait him out, but patience wasn't her strong suit. "I, um . . ."

"It'll take me about an hour to get there. Can you get to the house and lock yourself inside?"

"Actually, I have to get back to the café. How about if I leave the earring in a plastic bag on the counter, and you can pick it up whenever you get here?" She studied the pearl and gold piece of jewelry. Did it look familiar? Not that she could recall.

"There's no sign of Carter?"

She looked around. "No. He ran off the other way into the woods on the side of Miley's."

"Okay, then. Go ahead and do that. If I have questions, I'll either call or stop by the café. I'd prefer you not hang around there anyway."

She figured it best not to mention she planned to hang around long enough to pick up the garbage and bleach the scent off the top of the bin. It wouldn't take more than a few minutes. And if the fear in Carter's eyes was any indication, he'd probably stay long gone.

She stuffed the bear spray into her pocket, grabbed all the bags from the backseat and the keys from the ignition, then ran inside. The first thing she did when she reached the kitchen was drop the earring into a plastic bag and set it on the counter, then she shoved the perishables into the fridge and left the peppers and onions in a bag on the table. After that she donned rubber gloves, which she probably should have thought of before snatching the earring, and gathered the cleaning supplies she'd need. It only took a few minutes to clean up the mess Rocky had left behind, set a paver atop the can to hopefully keep him from getting back in, and wash her hands.

On her way out the door, she grabbed the bag of peppers and onions, paused to be sure the cameras were up and running, then locked up behind her and left. She connected her phone to the Bluetooth and hit Savannah's number.

Savannah picked up almost immediately. "Where are you? I was starting to get worried."

"I'm sorry, Savannah. Something came up, and I had to run home." Not a lie, and she would tell her the entire story as soon as she got back, but adding to the stress in her friend's voice now would serve no purpose. She stuffed the bear spray canister back into her purse, then started the car and backed out of the driveway, allowing one last lingering gaze at Miley's house while she pondered what had happened there. "I'm on my way back now, though. I picked up some fresh strawberries and blueberries. You want to hang out and watch a movie tonight?"

"Um. Yeah, I guess, that sounds okay."

As she passed the HOA office, Gia noted Irene's car still where she'd parked it. "Okay, sounds good. I'm gonna run. I'll see you in a few."

Gia disconnected without giving Savannah a chance to nix her plan. She rolled into the HOA lot, swung a U-turn so her car faced the road in case she had to make a quick exit, then got out and eased the door shut quietly. Even though she'd come up with an excuse for visiting on the fly, there was no need to announce her presence and give whomever might be with Irene a chance to hide.

She tried to look natural as she crossed the lot. Even if Carter had been the figure she'd seen with Irene, he was most likely long gone now. Of course, if it wasn't him, Irene might well still have company. She climbed the few front steps to the decking, then pulled the door open. The instant the air-conditioning hit her, with her clothes and hair still damp from getting caught in the rain and the sweat trickling down her back, goose bumps sprang up along her arms.

The reception area was empty, and she didn't bother to call out. Instead, she swung the half door open, eased it shut gently behind her, and started down the hallway toward Irene's office.

The sound of raised voices brought her up short. One of them was definitely a woman. Though she couldn't be sure it was Irene, she assumed it was since it was coming from her office. The other was male—and angry. Could Carter have made it back to the office so quickly? If he followed a straight line through the woods, it wouldn't take long at all.

Gia crept closer to the closed door with Irene's name on it and tried to keep an eye out as she pressed her ear against the door.

". . . enough of your whining, Scott. It's not helping anything, and I'm tired of listening to your sniveling."

When Gia had spoken to Irene, she'd seemed so sympathetic toward Scott that Gia had begun to wonder if they were having an affair, but whatever was going on in that office didn't sound like a lovers' spat.

"Yeah, well, if we don't find it, I'm going to get disbarred," Scott wailed.

"And I'm going to be in jail, so boo-hoo, and sorry I can't work up much sympathy for any inconvenience that might befall you," Irene shot back at the top of her lungs.

"Inconvenience? Seriously, Irene?" There was a pause, but when Scott spoke again, he seemed to have gained some control of himself. "You'd better watch out, Irene. And, if I were you, I'd sleep with one eye open. Keep in mind, jail isn't the worst thing that could happen to you."

As far as parting shots went, that was a doozy. Which meant Gia needed to hightail it out of there before he accentuated the threat by storming out and slamming the door. She bolted down the hallway and out the door, didn't even bother to look over her shoulder as she jumped into her car and tore out of the lot.

Tremors tore through Gia. Her hands shook wildly as she dialed Hunt. Why would Irene end up in jail? For murder? Or had she committed some other crime? And why would Scott be disbarred? It had to have something to do with Gladys blackmailing them. So, what were they looking for, and how could Gia find it before they did? And, the biggest question of all, had Scott just threatened Irene's life? Or had he simply reminded her of what could happen if she ended up on the killer's radar?

Chapter Sixteen

After dropping the peppers and onions off in the kitchen, Gia sat at the café counter and sipped her coffee, but it did little to ward off the chill that had gripped her since leaving Irene's office. She'd already spoken to Hunt, who'd promised to be in touch once he spoke to Irene and Scott and found Carter. Then, she'd updated Savannah, who leaned, arms folded, on the counter directly across from her; Alfie, who'd taken a stool on one side of her with his tablet in front of him; and Cole, who sat on her other side nursing a mug of coffee.

Savannah tapped her powder blue nails against the counter, the rhythmic *tap tap tap* grating on Gia's already raw nerves. "So, what? You think Scott killed Gladys?"

Did she? "I don't know what to think."

"From the way you described what he said to Irene, I'd take it as a threat," Cole offered.

"Yeah? Ya think?" Savannah quirked a brow. "Because it felt more like a warning to me. As if he were reminding her what could happen. What do you think, Gia? You were actually there to gauge the nuances."

"I don't know. It was hard to tell. I was listening through a door, so I couldn't see their faces or read anything in their body language. Plus, even though I could make out the words, they were kind of muffled." She shrugged and ran a finger around the lip of her mug, frustrated with herself for ever getting involved in this mess in the first place. "It could have been a threat, but I think you might be right, Savannah. Even though he was yelling, it seemed more scared than mad, though there was plenty of anger too. He just seemed so frightened to me."

Cole frowned into his coffee. "You think he was just reminding her that something worse than jail could happen to her if she pursued whatever it was they were looking for?"

"Yeah, I guess." Though she was far from certain.

"But you have no idea what that something is?"

"Nope. None." Maybe she shouldn't have taken off so quickly. She'd assumed Scott would leave right after he'd warned Irene off, but he might well have stayed. She'd gotten scared and bolted when she should have played it cool, straightened, and waited to see what would get said next.

If anyone opened the door, she could have lifted her hand as if she'd been about to knock and told Irene she'd stopped in to ask about trash cans and if the Homeowners Association would consider providing better bear-resistant cans than those provided by the county. She already knew the answer, had researched it after she'd first moved in and again when Rocky had decided to make his home in the tree beside her garage, but Irene wouldn't know that.

"And what was Carter doing in Miley's garage? You think he was looking for whatever Scott and Irene were trying to find?" Alfie twisted back and forth on his stool at warp speed.

"Huh . . ." Gia hadn't thought of that. It did make sense, though. "Maybe Irene or Scott hired him to find whatever it is?"

Alfie stopped his stool so suddenly he almost fell off, then tapped his tablet screen.

Then Gia remembered she hadn't been the only one with news. In all the confusion over Scott and Irene, she'd forgotten about Savannah's phone call. "You never did tell me what the Bailey sisters had to say."

"Oh, right. Well . . ." she started dramatically. "Apparently, they heard from a friend of a friend of a close acquaintance . . ." Her eyes sparkled with humor. "That Irene Kellerman and Cindy Marx were very close friends. Supposedly, they were roommates in college and maintained that close relationship in all the years since."

Huh. "That would explain why Irene allowed Carter to live on the property out there."

"Maybe, but why would she make blackmail payments to Gladys because of that? To save her own skin because she might get fired?" Savannah straightened and tossed the rag she'd been using to wipe the counter into a bus pan. Since the café was empty but for the four of them, and they'd already locked up, there was no need for discretion.

Gia thought back over the conversation between Irene and Scott. "No, I think it was something more. Scott was worried about getting disbarred, but Irene blew off his concerns and said she could end up in jail."

"Do you think she killed Gladys?" Savannah began prepping

coffeepots for the morning.

"Even if she did, which I'm not discounting, especially since I found the heel prints and that earring by the crime scene, I didn't get the impression that was what she was referring to. I think Gladys was holding something over her head." But what sort of illegal activity could Irene be involved in?

"Like she was doing to everyone, it seems." Cole finished off his coffee and started to get up, but Savannah lay a hand on his wrist and took the mug from him, then slid it into the bin under the counter.

Alfie pulled up the suspect list they'd started at breakfast. "Maybe if we update our chart with the new information we found today, we can get a clearer idea of who might be the killer."

Gia glanced over the information they already had. "Who do you want to start with?"

He shrugged. "It doesn't matter. Scott, I guess. We originally thought his motive might be that he was disinherited, or that he didn't know he was disinherited and was hoping to gain a fortune, either of which might still be the case, though it seems there was something more going on there too."

"Right," Savannah agreed. "But it seems to me he would want to keep his head down, especially if Gladys had something on him that could get him disbarred. Why draw attention to yourself by contesting the will or arguing for the inheritance?"

"Unless she left something in her will that could hurt him," Gia suggested.

"Like what?"

Gia began to warm to the idea. "Who knows? Maybe a safe-deposit box or a flash drive or something like that with information on the people she was blackmailing. Surely, she wouldn't commit all of their indiscretions to memory."

"Why not?" Alfie asked. "That would be the best way to keep it all secret."

Of course, not everyone had a memory like Alfie, whose brain worked more like a computer. "You might be right, but still, we have no idea how many people she was blackmailing or how much information she had on any of them. But it does seem like she'd have kept track somehow."

A shiver raced through Gia at the thought that she could have ended up on that list. She thought back to that morning and something Gladys had said. "You know, I don't remember exactly what we were talking about, because I was so aggravated, but I remember Gladys tapping her head and saying she had everything stored there, but then she said she also had a physical copy stashed away, or something to that effect."

She wished she could summon the memory more clearly, but it just wouldn't come.

"So, you're probably on the right track then with the flash drive or safe-deposit box," Alfie said.

"And it would explain not only why Scott and Irene were looking for something, but why Carter was in her garage as well, whether he was looking for himself or someone else. Now that we have a connection between him and Irene, it kind of changes the dynamic a bit."

"All right, so let's boil it down to a list I can use to update my chart." Alfie scribbled furiously on the tablet with his stylus.

Savannah grabbed an order pad and pen from beside the register.

Gia used the basics Alfie had already listed as a guide. "Let's start with Scott then. He obviously has motive. When he spoke in the café, it seemed as if he'd just found out he wasn't named in her will, so that means he still could have killed her thinking he'd inherit. And the amount of money Gladys had accumulated would be a strong motivator. Plus, she had something else she was holding over his head. So, he has motive, but what about opportunity?"

"Yes! Or, at least, maybe. I can't believe I forgot to show you guys this in all the confusion." Alfie whipped out his phone, swiped a few times, and held it out to them. "I finished going through more of the footage from Gia's cameras. It took a while, considering it was hours' worth of footage, but I came across this from . . . uh . . . a couple of hours before Gladys was killed."

Gia watched as a man crept along the side lawn toward Miley's house. When he reached the back corner of the garage, mere feet from where the figure had emerged from the shadows to kill Gladys, he paused, glanced over his shoulder from beneath a dark-colored hood, then disappeared around the back of the house. When Alfie played it a second time, Gia still couldn't be sure who it was. Although she had to admit it could be Scott, it could also be almost anyone else. The two things she did note were that it was most likely a man and he did not have on spiked heels. "Hey, Alfie, could you bring up the other footage, when the attacker comes out of the bushes?"

He swallowed hard. "Sure. You don't think the guy I just showed you was Scott?"

"It could have been, but it could also have been Ben Stettler or Carter Marx or anyone else. I agree, it seems like a man, but I couldn't identify him from that video. Can you enhance it somehow?"

"I might be able to. I'll play with it when I'm done here, but I already sent it to Hunt, and I'm sure he'll have people right on it, if they haven't already found it, which he refused to either confirm or deny."

A smile tugged at Gia's lips.

Alfie held out the video of the attacker.

Gia sobered instantly as she took the phone from him and watched the figure emerge from the hedges, dressed all in black, using the shadows for concealment for as long as possible. There was no way to tell what kind of shoes the person wore. It was also impossible to glean much else about the figure from their gait since the movements were stealthy and smooth. Designed to conceal the person's identity? The only thing she knew for sure was that the path the person followed did not match the heel marks she'd found. "You know what I was thinking? What was Gladys even doing out there in the middle of the night?"

Alfie shrugged and looked around at the others. "She must have come out the back of the house, or maybe the back of the garage."

"The same garage door Carter emerged from today." Had the killer thought she'd secreted information in the garage? If it was Carter, or the killer had paid Carter, it was possible he'd seen her emerge from the garage door and assumed she'd kept some record there. "She almost had to have known her assailant, don't you think? So, what would have lured her out at that hour? And, come to think of it, she must have gone out the front door since it was standing open the following morning when I called Hunt. Remember?"

"Maybe she was meeting someone for a payment, went out the front door and walked around to be sure there would be no witnesses," Savannah answered right away.

"Or to discuss future payments," Cole added. "Maybe she was

meeting with a potential victim, called him or her, told them she'd unearthed skeletons they'd want to keep buried, asked them to meet her when no one would be around."

That not only seemed possible, but likely. "So, where was Miley? Sleeping? Miley had already tossed Elijah out by then, so he wouldn't have been home."

Savannah leaned against the back counter and folded her arms over her chest. "You notice she threw Elijah out but not Gladys. Why would she have let her stay? I wouldn't have."

"No?" Gia couldn't say why that surprised her, but it did. Savannah was the sweetest, most caring person she'd ever met. But she could be a pit bull when anyone messed with her loved ones. "You'd have tossed them both?"

She studied Gia for a moment, seemed to weigh her words carefully. "You know, when I think about it in generic terms, my automatic instinct is to say yes. But if I try to make it more specific and imagine you'd betrayed me like that, I can't honestly say I would. I'd be hurt, devastated, angry, but I don't know that I'd toss you in the street without anywhere to go."

Gia studied Savannah, tried to think objectively. It didn't help that she was dating Savannah's cousin, or that she couldn't even imagine loving anyone other than Hunt, but she didn't think she'd throw Savannah out. They had too much history together, had been through too many good times, too many bad times, to simply walk away from her. They were sisters, just like Miley and Gladys. She could understand why Miley would have let Gladys stay, even if only until she found somewhere else to live. Plus, Gia hadn't seen Miley around the house. It was possible she'd left Gladys at the house and gone to stay with friends. Actually, the more she thought on that, the more she believed that's exactly what Miley had done. Because it's probably what Gia would have done.

But what about Elijah? Were he and Miley staying together somewhere? Would Gia have divorced her ex if he'd only been cheating on her and not cheating his clients, and some of his closest friends, out of millions? Maybe. Either way, she was fairly confident Elijah was history. She'd have to remember to ask the Bailey sisters if they knew.

"Maybe she felt more betrayed by her husband." Gia spoke softly, the memory of exactly what that betrayal felt like still an occasional raw wound.

Instinctually knowing where Gia's mind had gone, Savannah lay a hand over hers. "Or maybe she got rid of Elijah and kept Gladys around because she planned to kill her."

The thought brought a small wave of nausea. Could Miley have killed her own sister? "You know, I assumed Irene lost the earring, because she was wearing a pearl necklace on the video, and I think I remember her wearing pearl earrings, though I can't be positive. But I distinctly remember Miley was wearing pearl earrings when she came into the café, though I can't say with any certainty that the one I found matches those she had on."

"All right. So . . ." Alfie stood with his tablet and started to pace. "We have Irene Kellerman, who was hiding the fact that some of the Rolling Pines residents weren't adhering to the rules of conduct. Also, the fact that she may or may not have done something illegal Gladys may or may not have found out about and been blackmailing her over. Either way, we do know Gladys was blackmailing her. So, motive for Irene, check."

Gia bit back a smile. It seemed Alfie had missed his calling. He should have been Sherlock Holmes with tech.

"Then, we have the elusive Carter Marx, who has fled the crime scene not once but twice so far now." He held up two fingers. "And we know Gladys not only knew he was living on the land out there, but when she couldn't find any other way to get him evicted, she bought the property for the sole purpose of throwing him off."

Cole swung his stool around to face Alfie and leaned back against the counter. "But would that really be a motive for murder?"

"I've seen people murdered for less," Alfie shot back. "Of course, that was only in movies or on TV shows, but they're supposed to mimic real life, right?"

This time, Gia lost her battle, and the laugh blurted out. "I agree a hundred percent, Alfie."

He resumed his pacing. "So, that's Irene and Carter, both with motive, both with possible opportunity, since both live in Rolling Pines and would probably have been in residence at the time of the murder."

Gia couldn't argue that point, considering most people were home in bed at two in the morning. "What about Scott? He doesn't live in Rolling Pines, but I suppose he could have parked his car down the road and walked to Miley's."

Alfie tapped his stylus against his lips. "Good. That's good. And possibly being disbarred and losing his job would definitely rate high on my motive list."

Savannah's eyes went wide.

"Oh, wait. I didn't mean it that way. I didn't mean *I* would kill someone for that, I just meant . . ."

She laughed and let him off the hook. "I'm just messin' with you, Alfie."

He huffed and ran his hand over the buzz cut he couldn't seem to get used to.

Gia relaxed. Even though they were discussing murder, being with friends eased her fears and her anxiety. The tension began to seep out of her, and a warm sense of peace filled her.

"Okay, so that leaves us with Miley, who certainly had opportunity and motive, considering she lived with Gladys and the woman cheated with her husband."

"If you ask me"—Cole lifted a finger—"that would be a strong motive, especially after she took her in."

Alfie shook the stylus at him. "And I agree, but then I go back to Ben Stettler, who came over to Gia's to discuss Gladys's visit, offered to speak with the police on Gia's behalf, and just happened to leave out the fact that Gladys may have been blackmailing him too, even if I didn't find evidence of it. It's possible he paid cash to keep her quiet about him running the automotive shop on his property."

"And as far as evidence goes," Gia reminded them, "that hammer sure is incriminating."

They all nodded agreement on that, especially considering both his and Gladys's blood type had been found on the hammer, assuming the second blood type was his even if Hunt hadn't specifically said it was.

Savannah shook her head. "Although I doubt he'd have dropped a pearl earring at the crime scene. That had to have been Miley or Irene."

"That may be true, but from the video I just watched, I'm positive the track the killer took did not match up with the heel imprints in the dirt. Plus, no way would the police have missed that earring. Not noticing a notepad that had slid behind a table on the front porch is one thing, missing a piece of jewelry only half buried in the mud at the actual crime scene is something else entirely."

Savannah scoffed. "I can tell you one thing for sure. Knowing Hunt as well as I do, if one of the techs missed something that obvious, they probably wouldn't have a job tomorrow."

Gia couldn't argue that. Unfortunately, none of the information they'd amassed gave her any more insight into who the killer could be. Nor did it exonerate anyone. Which meant there was still a killer lurking around Rolling Pines, and it was time to pick up Thor and go home.

Chapter Seventeen

Thor stuck his head between the car seats from where he sat behind Gia and Savannah and nuzzled Gia's cheek.

She reached up absently to cradle his head and weaved her fingers into his fur. "I missed you too, boy."

Savannah, seemingly lost in thought as she stared out the window, scratched his head without turning.

Gia released him. "Sit back, now, boy."

He sulked as he dropped onto the backseat.

"Don't worry, Thor. We'll be together all night. I'm going to stay home and eat dessert and watch funny movies that won't remind me of murder."

Savannah didn't respond, just continued to stare at the acres of forest as they passed.

Gia tilted her head back and forth, working to ease some of the tension gathered in her neck. She could speak freely, since Alfie had asked Cole to drop him off at home, but without knowing what was on Savannah's mind, she had no clue what to say to her, how to ease whatever stress was plaguing her. She was just glad Savannah had agreed to come home with her. No way did she want to leave her alone without knowing what was wrong—because she had no doubt something was.

She hoped Gladys's murder hadn't stirred memories she'd worked hard to get past. But she wouldn't blame her if the fact that a murderer was roaming free in Rolling Pines had her on edge. It certainly had Gia unnerved, to put it mildly. "What do you want to do for dinner?"

"Um, I'm not going to stay for dinner. Thank you, but Leo said he's going to get off early, so we're going to go home and have a date night."

"That's great." And hopefully it would perk her up and help take her mind off her troubles. Then a thought occurred. Could Savannah and Leo be having problems? The two had been in love practically their whole lives, though it had taken Savannah a little while to figure that out. And Leo had given her the time and space she'd needed, while he'd waited patiently. "Are you and Leo doing okay?"

"Sure, why?" She watched the forest pass by out the passenger window, not sparing Gia so much as a glance.

"Just making sure." And with that, she ran out of conversation. Which had never once happened since the day she'd met Savannah. Even when they'd briefly shared an apartment in New York City when Savannah had moved up there to pursue a career as a dancer, they'd never been at a loss for something to say to each other. Nor had their silences ever been awkward or uncomfortable. Until today. "Savannah, you're not mad at me for anything, are you?"

"What?" She did turn then, her eyes wide. "What on earth would ever make you think that?"

"You're just so quiet. And I'm worried about you." Usually, Gia was the one to fall quiet, and Savannah could prattle on about anything all night long. "You're not acting like yourself. You do know you can talk to me about anything, right? And if you want me to keep it to myself, I will, just like I always have. That won't change just because I'm going to marry your cousin."

"Oh, Gia." Savannah reached out and clutched her hand. "I'm so sorry. I didn't mean to freeze you out or hurt your feelings."

Gia squeezed back, glad for the contact. "I'm not worried about my feelings, Savannah, I'm concerned about your well-being."

"Gia, I'm fine. Happier than a pig in mud. I promise. I've just been feeling a little out of sorts lately. That's all. First all the fuss with Gladys, then her murder. I just need a minute to get my bearings. And just being with you helps, even if I'm not quite up to talking, so thank you for that."

Gia studied her another moment, searched for sincerity in her eyes, and breathed a sigh of relief. "Just know, if you ever need me, I'm here."

"Honey, of that I have no doubt."

She hit the turn signal, despite the fact that there wasn't another vehicle around for miles, and turned into Rolling Pines feeling lighter than she had all day. "Do you want to come home with me until Leo gets off, or should I drop you off at home?"

"Uh, maybe just . . ." She pointed out the side window. "Do you see that?"

Gia lifted her foot off the accelerator and leaned forward to peer through the windshield. "See what?"

"The lights on at Miley's." Savannah opened her window and tilted her head for a better look. "The crime scene tape is still up, but I'd swear I just saw someone moving around inside."

"All right." Instead of pulling into her driveway, Gia drove past the house, trying to see into Miley's front window. No use, the curtains were pulled tightly shut. She drove all the way to the end of the block, made a U-turn, and then sat idling with the car still in gear. Her gaze bounced from the windshield to the rearview mirror to the sideview mirror and back again, searching for any sign of shadows moving out of the brush. "You know what? I'm just going to give Hunt a call and let him decide if he wants to have someone check it out."

She left the car in drive and kept her foot on the brake in case they had to move in a hurry. Surveilling their surroundings, she was just debating whether to leave a message or hang up and call Leo instead when he picked up.

"Hey, Gia." The background chaos alerted her that he hadn't yet left the station. That, and the fact that she could tell he was distracted. "What's going on?"

Okay, so quick and to the point. "Did you guys leave the lights on at Miley Davis's house?"

"No, why?" The background noise subsided as he must have pushed his door shut or stepped out of the fray. Maybe this was more of a problem than she realized.

Her heart rate kicked into overdrive. She eased off the brake, rolling slowly down the block. She tried to peer into the windows as she passed the house again, then pulled into her own driveway. She still didn't see anything, and felt a little foolish calling in the cavalry, but it was important to her that Savannah know she'd always take her concerns seriously. Besides, the situation also seemed to have piqued Hunt's interest. "Because we were just getting home, and Savannah noticed the lights on and thought she saw a shadow moving around inside."

"Hang on."

Gia listened to the muffled sound of Hunt's voice as she waited for him to get back to her. "Come on, Thor. Let's get you inside."

Savannah got out of the passenger side, then glanced quickly toward the Davis house before heading straight for Gia's front door.

Gia waited for Thor to do his business then hurried after her. By the time he was done, Savannah had already unlocked the front door and stood staring anywhere but at Miley's house as she held the door open.

When Hunt resumed the call, there was no mistaking the tension in his voice. "Are you two in the house?"

"Not yet. We're just walking in."

"Get inside and lock the doors. Stay put until you hear back from me."

"Okay. Is something wrong?"

"Leo is almost there. He left early, so he's only a few minutes out. I'm leaving now. Just stay inside, and keep Thor in, until we find out if anyone is in the house, okay?"

Perhaps the circumstances were more dire than she realized. "Sure."

"Is Savannah with you?" The *ding ding ding* in the background meant he'd already reached his vehicle.

She barely resisted the urge to look across the street, worried now that she'd alert someone to their interest. *If* anyone was even in there. "Yes. She's already inside."

"Good. Just give us a few minutes to check it out. I'll call you back or Leo will stop in to pick Savannah up after he checks."

"All right." She checked to make sure Savannah had already headed for the kitchen with Thor. "Thanks for checking it out, Hunt. I didn't see anything, but Savannah was very sure about it, and I don't want to give her any more reason to be frightened."

"No worries. You know I would do anything for Savannah. Besides, she's extremely observant, so it's very possible she did see something."

"Plus, the lights shouldn't be on, so there's that." Gia held her breath until she slammed the door shut behind her. She turned the dead bolt. "Okay, we're locked up tight."

"Okay, I'll see you in about half an hour. We can go out to dinner if you'd like."

"I'm looking forward to it." And she found she really was. A quiet peaceful evening with Hunt was just what she needed to help her unwind. Maybe she'd heat up some leftovers instead of going out, though. The last thing she wanted to do was sit around listening to more gossip. Speaking of listening . . . She opened the scanner app on her phone so she'd hear the all-clear go out once Leo had finished checking Miley's house.

She set the phone on the table. "Do you want something to drink?"

"Nah, I'm good." Savannah pulled a chair out and sat, propped her elbows on the table, and cradled her head in her hands. "Are you going to feed Thor yet?"

"Not yet. I turned on the scanner so we'll know when the house has been cleared. I'll wait to feed him then since I can't take him out yet." Gia sat across from her. "You okay?"

"Yeah. Just a killer headache." She slid her fingers through her hair and squeezed the strands.

"You want—"

"No, thanks. I'm good." She lifted her head, leaned back in the chair, and folded her arms. Dark circles ringed her eyes. Long strands of blonde hair had escaped her bun to frame her face. And while all of those indications were unusual for Savannah, it was the nail she'd chipped hours earlier and hadn't even bothered to file that pinged Gia's radar. "Look, Savannah, I know you keep saying you're fine. And I'll admit it's probably getting annoying to keep having me ask if you're okay over and over again."

She grinned, and for a moment she seemed like herself again. "You could at least try to switch up the phrasing for variety. Didn't they teach that in the schools up in New York?"

"Now that you mention it, I do recall something about that. Unfortunately, it's been a few years since school."

She quirked a brow and laughed. "A few?"

"Ha ha." But her hopes soared. Maybe her friend was fine, and Gia was making more of her just being tired than there really was. "All right, all right. I'll leave you alone for now. Just please know if you ever need me, I'm here. No matter what."

"Noted and appreciated. Thank you, Gia. Knowing you have my back means more to me than you'll ever know. And, actually . . ." She scooted forward, perched on the edge of her seat, and sighed. "There has been something on my mind all day, and I'm going to need—"

Three loud pops from the front of the house interrupted whatever she'd been about to say, and Savannah lurched to her feet, tumbling the chair behind her. There was no mistaking the sound of gunfire.

Thor started to bark and bolted for the front window.

Gia reached for her cell phone as she stood.

Before she could grab it, Savannah shoved her hand into her purse and came out with the pistol she'd taken to carrying after she'd been attacked.

"No! Savannah, you stop right there."

The world needed to stop for one second. She had to call Hunt. Had to stop Savannah. Thor was going ballistic. In the fraction of a second it took all of those thoughts to race through her mind, Savannah shoved past her.

Taking the phone with her, Gia ran down the hallway after Savannah, somehow made it to the front door ahead of her, and blocked her path. When she reached out, she fumbled the phone and it dropped. "Savannah, please. You don't know what's going on. It might just be hunters. We have to call Hunt, and I can't do that if you go charging out of here. Please, just hold on one second and hand me the phone, then I'll go with you. I promise. I told you I'd always have your back, and I will, but I'm begging you, just let me call for help first."

"Fine." Tears streamed down her face, and her hand trembled as she picked up the phone and handed it to Gia. "Make it fast. I have to get to him, Gia."

"I know, and if he needs help—"

The scanner came to life, and Gia held her breath and prayed. But it wasn't Leo's voice that came over, it was Ben Stettler's. "Hey, can anyone hear me? You have an officer down out here. I repeat, officer down!"

"No! Leo!" Savannah's eyes rolled up, then closed as her legs buckled, and she went down.

Gia caught her and cradled Savannah in her arms as she sank to the floor with her back against the door.

Chaos erupted from the scanner, and she barely registered Hunt's voice issuing orders amid the flurry of activity. For the first time, it did nothing to alleviate her fears.

Thor barked from next to her ear, licked her face, then dropped to the floor beside them and whimpered.

Tears streamed from Gia's eyes. She rocked Savannah back and forth, praying there was some sort of mistake yet knowing there wasn't. Blackness encroached from both sides, tunneling her vision. She'd promised Savannah she'd always be there for her. And the moment she needed her most had come. Gia would not fail her. She would not give up. She refused to relinquish her desperate hold on consciousness.

Leo had been shot, and Gia had to pull herself together, get Savannah up, and get to him. Now.

Chapter Eighteen

"Savannah!" Gia shifted position, laid Savannah on the cool terra-cotta tile, and knelt over her. She tapped her cheek. As much as she wanted to hold her, comfort her, ease her pain, she couldn't. There was no time. "Savannah, you have to get up. Right now."

Savannah moaned.

Gia reached over and shut the scanner off. As much as she wanted to keep track of what was happening, no units had yet reached Leo, and she needed to get out there. If she couldn't rouse Savannah, she'd have to leave her with Thor. "Savannah!"

Her eyes fluttered open, then she squinted at Gia. For one instant, her eyes were filled with confusion. It was quickly replaced by sheer terror as she lurched upright, grabbed her head, and rocked unsteadily. "Leo?"

Gia gripped her shoulders, knelt facing her. "Savannah, listen to me. I have to get to Leo. Ben Stettler made the call, but we don't know if he's with him, if he's administering any first aid. I want you to wait—"

"No! I'm fine. Go. I'll be right behind you."

As much as she wanted to argue, to insist Savannah stay put where it was safe, there was no time. And no point. Gia understood her friend well enough to know that. Instead of wasting precious time arguing, she grabbed the gun that had clattered to the floor when Savannah had gone down, unlocked the front door, then slid out without letting Thor, Klondike, or Pepper escape.

She scanned the yard and street as she moved, weapon held in front of her, finger alongside the trigger outside the guard. She'd been to the range with Savannah, at her insistence, and knew how to use the weapon, but she was far from comfortable with it.

A form she assumed was Ben Stettler was hunched over and performing CPR on another form lying still on the ground.

Giving up any semblance of control, she bolted across the street and dropped beside them. She tucked the gun into the waistband at her back. Onlookers had already begun to gather, and Ben had been there for at least a minute or two, though it seemed like hours, and no one had yet taken another shot, so she shoved the fact that an active shooter could still be present aside. "Ben?"

Ben looked up, sweat pouring down his face, and continued chest compressions. He paused long enough to rip off his T-shirt and hand it to Gia. "Press that against the wound."

"One wound?"

"Yes, as far as I can tell."

"But I heard three shots." She did as instructed, balling up the yellow fabric and pressing it against Leo's chest. Blood soaked it almost immediately.

"Press harder, Gia," Ben huffed.

She leaned over, using her weight to try to stem the flow. "Do you know what you're doing, Ben?"

"Yes, ma'am." He sucked in a breath. "I was an EMT. You just do what I tell you and we're going to save this boy."

"Okay. All right." She shoved aside the tears blurring her vision with her arm. She heard Savannah sobbing behind her. Then the sobs retreated as someone must have moved her farther away, whispering urgently about giving them room to work.

A guy she didn't know tapped Ben's shoulder. "Take a break."

He nodded, switched places with the guy, then swiped an arm across his brow.

A woman held her cell phone out to him. "The dispatcher wants an update."

"Got it." He took the phone from her and started checking Leo's vitals and rattling off a bunch of stuff Gia couldn't wrap her head around at the moment, none of which sounded promising.

Sirens wailed in the distance, bringing a wave of relief.

A teenage boy in sweats and open work boots dropped to his knees beside her. "You want I should take over?"

"Um." But she had to do this, couldn't hand his care over to anyone else. "I've got it, thank you, but could you please check on my friend. She's got blonde hair, and she was wearing . . . uh . . ." She drew a total blank.

"It's all right." The boy patted her shoulder. "My mom's got her. She's upset, but she seems okay. Someone just gave her water, and someone else brought a lawn chair for her to sit down. My dad and some of the other guys have set up a perimeter in case the shooter is still around. Wait . . ."

Gia tried to process everything he was telling her. Even though all of it didn't sink in, the idea that everyone in the community was pitching in to help, and Savannah was being taken care of, was all she needed to comprehend. She lifted one hand long enough to brush the side of Leo's too pale cheek. "Please, Leo. You have to fight. Please. For Savannah. She needs you."

"Hold up." Ben gripped the wrist of the guy who'd taken over CPR. He pressed two fingers against Leo's neck. "We've got a pulse!"

Gia sagged with the relief that rushed through her. Every inch of her body prickled with adrenaline. The instant she realized her muscles had relaxed, she tightened them, being sure to maintain pressure.

A cheer went up from those gathered, and Gia chanced a quick look up. Not only had these people come together and helped, their expressions were filled with emotion. Tears streaked too many faces to count, several groups held hands and continued to pray, and others looked on as they surrounded Savannah and showered her with support.

Savannah sat, eyes glued to Gia, visibly shaking.

Gia forced a smile and nodded encouragement before returning her attention to Leo.

Then, the sea of onlookers parted as the first emergency vehicles arrived.

Hunt's SUV fishtailed around the corner, sirens blaring, and barely rocked to a stop before he jumped out and ran to them. He dropped beside Gia. "How bad?"

Ben met his stare and gave one curt head shake.

"Okay." He gripped Gia's wrist, squeezed, and stood. Instead of going to Savannah, as she'd expected he might, he started moving the crowd back. She had no doubt that, like her, once he went to her, he'd lose the battle for control of his emotions. "I need anyone who saw what happened here to step forward. Everyone else, can we back up across the street, please."

A few people moved forward with none of the hesitation Gia might have expected, and Hunt pulled out a notepad, his hands shaking, and dropped his pen. Before he could bend to pick it up, a guy grabbed it and held it out to him.

The ambulance arrived, drawing Gia's attention away from Hunt and the investigation. All that mattered to her right now was Leo and Savannah. First, they'd get through this, and then they'd figure out who did this and make sure they went to prison.

As more officers arrived, they cast worried glances toward Leo, then took over crowd control for Hunt and joined the men guarding the perimeter. A paramedic took over for her, checked the wound, and replaced her makeshift compress with something more suitable.

She backed out of the way, still on her knees, eyes focused on Leo.

The same teen boy hooked her beneath one arm and helped her to her feet. "Come on. I went and put a chair for you by your friend."

"Thank you." Gia brushed her knees off, more for something to do than interest in her appearance. Plus, she needed one moment to gather herself, to rein in her fear and any uncertainty that might show in her eyes, before consoling Savannah.

She stopped beside Hunt, who was interviewing an older woman with a Yorkie clutched in one arm while the other gestured wildly as she spoke. "Excuse me, Hunt. I'm sorry to interrupt, but can Savannah and I go to the hospital? You can meet us there to take our statements."

"Of course." He glanced past her. "How is he?"

She shrugged. "Ben says he's got a good chance of making it, and the paramedics seemed to agree."

"Good." He looked away and stared into the distance, where there was nothing to see but the forest enshrouded in darkness, then swiped a hand over his five-o'clock shadow. "Yeah. You go take care of Savannah, and I'll be there as soon as I can."

She didn't bother telling him to find whoever did this, because she already knew he would. Instead, she simply turned and walked away.

Before she reached Savannah, a woman stopped her and held out a water bottle, then tipped her head toward Gia's hands.

Gia swallowed hard, then nodded her thanks and held her hands out while the woman used the water to wash Leo's blood away, then someone else handed her a towel. All she could manage was a raspy, whispered, "Thank you."

When she finally reached Savannah, she said nothing, simply helped her stand and pulled her into her arms. She held her close, rocked and cried with her, smoothed her hair off her face. She closed her eyes and took a moment to pray Leo would heal, to say thank you for everyone who'd come out to help save him and protect him. Then she sniffed, took a tissue someone handed her, and kept an arm around Savannah. "Come on, hon. We have to get to the hospital. They're putting Leo in the ambulance now, if you want to ride with him."

She nodded, and Gia guided her to the ambulance. "I'll follow you there."

"Thank you." She started to get into the ambulance, then paused and turned back to Gia. "Someone from the department will notify Leo's family, but could you please go tell my father what happened? And my brothers? Everyone will have heard an officer was hurt, but I don't want them to hear it was Leo from the gossipmongers."

"No problem, Savannah. I'll go right now, then I'll meet you. Will you be okay until I get there?"

She sniffed, nodded, then climbed into the back of the ambulance, took Leo's hand in hers, and pressed it against her lips.

The instant the doors shut, Gia ran across the street, weaving through the crowd to reach her front door. She grabbed her cell phone from where it had dropped on the floor. Savannah would need her purse, so she put the gun she'd forgotten about back inside and set it beside the front door. As much as she wanted to run right out, it would no doubt be a long night, and Thor needed to be taken care of. As did Klondike and Pepper. She grabbed her own bag, then Savannah's, and stopped to ruffle Thor's fur, hug him tight, then locked the door behind her and dialed Zoe's number as she ran to the car without glancing over at the crime scene. There was no need. That vision would be ingrained in her memory forever.

"Gia? Is everything okay?"

"No, um, Zoe . . ." With no hope of controlling her emotions any longer, a sob tore free.

"Gia? What happened?" Her voice faded as she shifted away from the phone. "Trevor, come quick. Something's wrong with Gia."

"Gia?" The concern in Trevor's voice only made it harder to pull herself together.

She sobbed softly, sucked in deep greedy breaths, then finally found a way to speak. "Leo's been shot. It's bad, Trevor."

"Oh, no. Where's Savannah?"

"On her way to the hospital." She inhaled another deep, shaky breath. "She went with him in the ambulance."

Zoe must have been listening in, because she started crying softly. Trevor only took a moment to console her. "What do you need from us?"

"They didn't find the shooter yet, and I don't want to leave Thor here alone, but I have to go to Savannah's father and brothers, then get to the hospital. Is there any way you guys can come get Thor, Klondike, and Pepper while there's still plenty of officers around?" There wasn't much she could do for Savannah now, but she would see to it her little gray and white tabby cat was safe.

"Pepper's at your house?"

"Yes."

"We're on our way."

"Thank you."

"Don't even mention it. Just do what you have to and get to Savannah. We'll take care of everything else."

More grateful than she could ever remember being, for the home and the community she was now part of, Gia disconnected the call and dropped her cell into the cupholder. Then she spent the half hour ride to Mr. Mills's house crying her eyes out and vowing to somehow find whoever had hurt Leo.

Chapter Nineteen

It didn't take long to notify Savannah's father, who assured Gia he'd contact his sons and meet her at the hospital. Then he'd ushered her out quickly so she could return to Savannah's side. By the time she reached the hospital parking lot, she had herself somewhat back together. Her emotions had run full circle from fear, to sadness, to anger, which slowly simmered until it had boiled over into full-on rage. Now, fear once again gripped her as she slung her bag over her shoulder, locked the car, and hurried across the parking lot.

How dare anyone shoot Leo? He was one of the kindest, sweetest men she'd ever known. He would do anything for anyone and had the patience of—

A shadow emerged from behind a white van and fell over her. She froze, stiffened, bombarded by images from the video of Gladys's abduction. She should run, scream, fight. She had only a fraction of a second to realize her mistake as someone grabbed her from behind and clasped a hand over her mouth. Hot breath rushed over her neck, and the scent of garlic turned her stomach. "Where is it?"

Where's what? But his hold was too tight for her to voice the question. She gripped a thick arm, turned her face away from him, and tried to squirm out of her attacker's grasp, searching for some way to suck in enough air to scream if she could manage to free herself.

His grip only tightened. His? Yes, definitely a man.

"Listen to me." The harsh whisper against her ear coiled her stomach.

Familiar? She couldn't be sure. Nausea threatened.

He started to drag her toward the van. "You're going to get into the van, take me to wherever the book is hidden, and then I will release you."

Yeah, right. Terror had her breathing too hard through her nose. Spots of light danced before her eyes. She needed air.

"You have to understand." He wheezed out a strangled breath. "I can't let you go until you give me the book. You could lie about it"—*wheeze*—"then, as soon as I leave"—*wheeze*—"you'll just tell Hunt."

Everything in her went still at the mention of Hunt's name. Not Captain Quinn, not even Detective Quinn, or simply the police, but

Hunt. This was someone she knew. Or at least someone who knew her. The thought cleared the haze of panic, allowed her to think more clearly.

He held her tight against his body as he rounded the van.

No way could she let him get her inside, no matter who he was. She'd already messed up, should have paid better attention to her surroundings. She'd been crossing a dark parking lot, alone, and should have been more aware. Instead of taking the safest, well-lit route, she'd weaved her way between cars in the most straightforward path to Savannah. A costly mistake. She wouldn't make another.

"I know you have it. I saw her carry it to your house." *Wheeze, wheeze* . . . "When she left, it wasn't in her hands." When her attacker lifted her, tried to wrestle her into the van's cargo area, she planted her feet against the back bumper and shoved with all her might.

He stumbled back, hit the front of an SUV, and grunted. His hold loosened just enough.

She spun toward him, catching him by surprise, and slammed her head into his face.

He staggered back but quickly regained his footing. Before she could make any attempt to escape, he grabbed a handful of her hair and slammed her head against the van's door.

Stunned, she fell to her knees, dropping her purse, whose contents spilled across the lot. If only she'd thought to bring Savannah's purse instead of leaving it locked in the car. Could she get back to the car, reach the weapon? Even if she could, could she point it at someone and pull the trigger?

She tried to crawl away, her hands and knees stinging as the blacktop scraped them raw.

Her attacker grabbed her again, around the waist, tried to hoist her up. "I'm sorry, but I can't . . ."

Then she spotted the bear spray Hunt had given her rolling toward the van's back wheel. Giving up the fight, she grabbed the canister and let the man yank her to her feet. When he shoved her once again toward the gaping back doors and certain death, she whirled on him, held her breath, squeezed her eyes closed, and remembered to flip the safety before fully depressing the plunger.

He coughed and sputtered as he staggered backward to get away from the spray.

"Hey! What's going on over there?" A man's voice. Close.

Trying to keep her attacker in sight as tears streamed down her face and her vision blurred, Gia lurched to the side, desperate to put any distance between her and the van. She caught her balance against the side of a MINI Cooper.

Her attacker tumbled into the back of the van. "Go! Go! Go!"

The tires screeched as the driver floored it and rocketed across the lot.

Footsteps pounded toward her.

The license plate. She needed to get . . . But she couldn't make it out through the tears the pepper spray had elicited before the driver whipped out of the lot, swinging one of the back doors shut.

Someone wrapped an arm around her, gripped her elbow.

She swung, fought, tried to turn the empty canister toward whoever it was.

"Gia? Gia. Hey. It's okay, honey." His grip tightened as he struggled to calm her. "It's Cole. I've got you."

Cole? What are you doing here? But when she sucked in a breath to ask, pepper spray burned her throat. She coughed, violently, and bent at the waist to get enough air.

Without loosening his hold, he turned to someone over his shoulder. "Cybil, go for help."

"I already called 911." She laid a warm hand on Gia's arm. "Gia, let us care for you now. You're safe."

For some reason, the touch soothed, and she sagged into Cole's arms. The first time she'd met Cybil Devane walking through the forest alone, with her long, white-streaked dark hair and robe-looking cape, Gia had thought her some kind of mystic. Now, and not for the first time, she had to wonder again. There was definitely something calming about the older woman. She exuded reassurance, comfort, peace.

When Gia reached up to rub her eyes, Cole gently pushed her hands away. "No, that'll only make it worse."

Cybil uncapped a water bottle and held it out to him. "Here, rinse her eyes."

Cole took the bottle, poured blessedly cool water over her eyes and face. He eased her against a nearby car, helped her to balance against the front bumper, then stepped back to examine her. "Just take it easy, hon. You're panicked more than anything. Take a few deep breaths, and just keep your eyes closed for a few minutes."

She did as he said, taking slow, deep breaths of the hot, thick air scented with night-blooming jasmine. Tremors tore through her, threatening to buckle her legs.

Then, in an instant, they were surrounded by police and emergency personnel. When a couple of people lifted her onto a gurney, she barely protested. Instead, she asked them to raise the back so she could sit, leaned back, closed her eyes, and waited for the tremors to subside.

By the time the doctor had checked her over and her eyes had been flushed, she began to feel more like herself. But she had to open her eyes, get up off this gurney, and get to Savannah. She yanked the cool compress off and set it aside, then blinked her eyes a few times to bring her vision clear.

According to Cole, half of Boggy Creek was in the waiting room with Savannah, but Gia still needed to get to her. She hadn't heard from Hunt, nor had she expected to. Leo was not only one of his officers, but a very close friend, more like a brother, as well. Hunt wouldn't take a break until his assailant had been found.

Had the man that attacked her been Leo's shooter? It seemed likely. And yet . . . The guy hadn't seemed to know what he was doing. At the time, the entire scenario had been terrifying. She couldn't deny that. Still, looking back, he should have been able to take her. Easily. Especially when he had backup in the van. So, how had she escaped? While she'd love to think it was her wit and mad fighting skills that had saved her, she knew better. She'd been foolish to cut between cars in a dark parking lot with her mind centered a million miles away.

But her attacker had made mistakes too. For starters, he'd referred to Hunt by his nickname, alerting her that he was familiar with the police captain. Also, he said he'd seen Gladys holding the book at Gia's. So, who could have seen her? Ben Stettler had been there. She replayed the voice in her head, but she couldn't place it.

Ben was in good shape, though, despite the beer belly. He was always tinkering with something or another in the yard. She couldn't see him losing his breath so quickly. And, as strong as he'd seemed while holding her, the way he was huffing and puffing told her he might not have had as much strength as it had felt like in the moment.

Who else could it have been? Carter, maybe? Or Scott? And who was the accomplice in the van?

Then again, maybe he'd said someone else had seen Gladys holding the book. The driver, maybe?

Gia squeezed her eyes closed. Tears still leaked from the corners, but it didn't matter. It was time to get up and go see how Leo was doing and be there for Savannah. She'd leave the detecting to the police.

"So, there you are."

Gia's eyes shot open and she started to sit up.

"No, don't get up. Stay there." Savannah pushed her back then nudged her hip. "Just scoot over a bit."

"What are you doing here? How's Leo? Have you heard anything? Why aren't you with him?" Gia scooted over to give Savannah room to sit beside her. "I was just on my way—"

"Hey. Slow down." Savannah squeezed in next to Gia on the narrow gurney, put her feet up, and crossed her ankles. Then she tilted her head onto Gia's shoulder and clasped one of Gia's hands in both of hers. "Leo's still in surgery, but the doctors are optimistic. It'll still be a few hours before we hear anything."

Gia allowed the news to pour through her, easing some of the tension. She sank against the back of the gurney and tipped her head against Savannah's. "I'm so glad to hear that. He's going to be fine, Savannah."

"He has to be." She moved one hand to lay over her stomach. "I don't know what we'd do without him."

"Hey." Gia squeezed her hand tighter. "Don't even talk like that. I'm sure Leo will make a full recovery. He's strong, and he loves you enough to pull through by sheer willpower. But no matter what happens—Wait. What? We?"

Savannah nodded and sat up so she could face Gia. A soft sob escaped. "I'm pregnant. I think about three months. I didn't even realize it until the other day, and it suddenly dawned on me. So, I ran to the pharmacy for a test. I did one before we left your house, then another in the bathroom at the café, just to be sure, you know? And that plus sign popped up right away."

"Oh, Savannah." Gia pulled her into her arms, held her. A cascade of emotions threatened to suffocate her—joy, love, followed too closely by fear. "I am so thrilled for you. You are going to make the most amazing mommy."

She half laughed, half cried. "You think?"

"I don't think, I know." And she meant it with all of her heart. Savannah would be the perfect mother, patient, kind, so filled with love it was a wonder she didn't burst. "And Leo is going to be a great father."

Her gaze fell to her hands. "If he makes it."

"Do not talk like that. He's going to make it."

"But what if he doesn't, Gia? I didn't even tell him. My first instinct was to call him and tell him right away. I was so beyond thrilled, and I wanted him to be the first to find out, you know?"

She nodded, her heart shattering into a million pieces.

"But I didn't want to tell him over the phone. I wanted to make it special, do a date night, tell him out on the deck, beneath the stars, with the forest all around us, in the home where our new baby would live, and blossom, and grow. And now . . ." She sobbed the words out. "What if he dies without ever even knowing he was going to be a dad?"

"He *is* going to be a dad." Knowing there was no way to ease the pain gripping her, Gia simply held her, rocked with her, cried with her. When she finally got her wits about her, she set Savannah back, got up, and grabbed a box of tissues from the counter. "Here. Let's get you cleaned up and get back to the waiting room so you'll be right there when Leo comes out of surgery, and you can tell him the amazing news."

Savannah sniffed, wiped her eyes. "You really think he's going to pull through?"

"I absolutely do." Gia prayed hard that she was right. "And he's going to be so thrilled when he finds out."

After blowing her nose a few times, Savannah got up and tossed the tissues in the corner trash can. She offered a tentative smile through tears. "Well, eventually, he's going to be thrilled. First, he's going to be shocked."

Gia wrapped an arm around her best friend, pulled her close, and laughed. Leo was going to pull through. He had to. Especially now that he had even more incentive.

"But, just so you know, I'm not going to let up on pushing you to get married already. Remember that favor we discussed? I'm calling it in." They walked together, side by side, and Savannah beamed at Gia. "I want you guys to get married right away so we can have our babies together."

Gia tripped over her own feet and would have gone down if not for Savannah's quick reflexes. Or, perhaps she'd simply anticipated the reaction. All rational thought skidded to a stop. "Say what, now?"

Chapter Twenty

By four a.m., Gia was still reeling. She and Savannah sat quietly in the corner of the surgical waiting room, surrounded by so many friends and family they overflowed into the hallway.

Alfie sat on Gia's other side, crying softly and banging away on his laptop.

Cole and Cybil sat together nearby and had already checked to see if Gia was doing okay at least a hundred times. Even though she'd assured them an equal number of times that she was okay, the less-than-discreet glances Cole kept aiming at her didn't escape Gia's notice.

She shifted in her seat, restless from sitting still for so long, sore from the attack in the parking lot, and completely exhausted. She lay her head back and closed her eyes, then opened them a moment later and glanced at the clock on the wall—two minutes later than the last time she'd looked, and still no word from Leo's surgeon or from Hunt.

Savannah's family had come, and her dad sat on her other side, cradling her hand in his, patting her arm every so often and whispering reassurances. She hadn't told anyone else about her pregnancy, and had sworn Gia to secrecy, but Gia couldn't help being concerned with the amount of stress being placed on her right now. Yet, every time Gia brought up seeing a doctor, Savannah simply shook her head and refused to leave this spot until she knew Leo was safe.

Earl sat talking quietly with Trevor and Zoe, who'd come after bringing Thor, Klondike, and Pepper to Trevor's mansion and seeing they were safe and tended to. Earl's kids had come earlier, with their respective spouses and a pack of kids, but most had left after he'd assured them he'd be okay and would call them the instant there was news.

When Ben Stettler walked in, nodded to Savannah, and leaned against a wall in the corner, Savannah stood and went to him. She hugged him, thanked him for saving Leo, then clasped his hands and spoke quietly with him for a few moments.

When she returned to her seat, Gia took her turn. No way would she believe this man who'd worked so hard to save Leo had harmed him. Nor would she buy that he'd attacked her and tried to pull her into the van, no matter whose blood had been found on the hammer. "I don't know how I can ever thank you, Ben. Leo wouldn't have made it without you."

His cheeks flamed red. "I'm just glad I was there to help, and I'm sorry it took me so long to get here. I'd have come sooner but I had to stay and answer questions for the police. Not that I could tell them much."

"Can you tell me what happened, Ben?" It didn't matter that prying ears were everywhere, or that from where they stood near the doorway, there was no way to have a private conversation.

"I was working out back when I heard the gunshots go off. I had no doubt what they were, but to be honest, I wasn't too concerned, just annoyed because I figured someone was hunting too close to the development. I went out there to reprimand them and remind them that kids and pets live in the neighborhood, and they shouldn't be shooting so close. When I came around the corner of the house by Miley's, I saw . . ." His voice hitched, and his breathing turned ragged. He took a few deep breaths. "Leo's police vehicle was sitting in the driveway with the blue and red lights flashing and the headlights illuminating someone on the ground. As soon as I saw Leo, he became my first concern. I ran to him, realized how badly he'd been hurt, and called for help. Then I administered first aid until the ambulance arrived."

"You never saw the shooter?" Disappointment surged in her.

"No. I never saw anyone until people started coming out of their houses to see what was going on, probably initially drawn by the sound of gunshots but more so by the police car with the lights on."

Gia hugged him again. "Thank you, Ben."

"Sure thing. I just hope he's going to be okay."

"Yeah, me too." She returned to her vigil, sitting between Savannah and Alfie as they all waited for word.

Willow and Skyla rushed in, scanned the room, then hurried to Savannah the instant they spotted her. When Savannah stood, Willow threw her arms around her neck. "I'm so sorry, Savannah. Is there anything we can do?"

Savannah sniffed, tears streaming down her raw cheeks, and Gia handed her a tissue. "Not right now, but thank you for coming."

"Is there any word?" Skyla hugged her next while Willow continued to cling to her hand.

She shook her head. "Nothing yet."

Two men who'd been sitting across from them stood and offered Willow and Skyla their seats, then headed off to get coffee.

Willow finally released Savannah to hug Gia. "Are you okay?"

She frowned. Could word have spread to them already? "I'm good. How did you—?"

"Seriously? Boggy Creek is sizzling like a live wire right now. Mostly everyone who's not at the hospital is wide awake by their phones awaiting news."

A chill rushed through Gia.

"Sorry it took so long to get here. Mom and I stopped at the café. I hope it's okay . . ." She caught her lower lip between her teeth and glanced at Skyla, who stepped in for her own hug.

"It was my choice, Gia. I just figured with everything going on it was best to close for the day, so we went in and tended to whatever would need doing and put a sign on the door, not that all of Boggy Creek won't know what happened by opening time, but still . . . We accepted the morning delivery, and we didn't want to see all of the rolls and bagels and stuff go to waste, so when we explained to the driver what had happened, he offered to drop everything at the homeless shelter."

Tears pricked the backs of her eyes, and she struggled not to let them fall.

"But if you'd rather open," Willow offered, "we can go in and do that instead."

"No. Absolutely not." She wrapped her arms around Willow, hugging the young girl close, then gestured for her to sit. "I can't tell you how much I appreciate you guys going in and taking care of everything. To be honest, and I'm kind of ashamed to admit it, but I never even gave the café a second thought."

And it's not like she didn't realize how late, or early, it was, considering she'd checked the clock every couple of minutes. It just never occurred to her to be anywhere else but right where she was. Apparently, most of Boggy Creek agreed with her. And, while hushed conversations took place all around them, there was not a single morsel of gossip that Gia had heard so far. Even Estelle and Esmeralda Bailey sat quietly together awaiting word.

"It was no problem at all." Skyla squeezed Gia's arm then sat beside her daughter and set her pocketbook beneath her seat. "It's not easy to sit and do nothing. So, when we heard, we figured that's what we could do. And now, we'll sit and pray and wait with you."

Losing her battle with tears, Gia simply nodded.

"Hey, Gia." Alfie leaned his head close to hers, keeping his voice low. "I think I found something."

She glanced around the room to see if he'd been overheard, but everyone seemed to either be lost in their own quiet conversations or their own thoughts. Those who sat closest to them wouldn't repeat anything Alfie might say anyway, and it would be good to have something else to think about for a few minutes. "What's up?"

He twisted his laptop just enough so that she could see the screen without drawing any attention. When he tapped a key, rows of numbers popped up.

"What am I looking at?" she whispered.

"Irene Kellerman's motive for killing Gladys?"

She sat up straighter, studied the information on the screen again, but still couldn't decipher what she was looking at. "For real?"

"Yup." He hit another button and what looked like bank information scrolled across the screen. Then he pitched his voice even lower. "She was embezzling money from the HOA. A lot of money."

"Are you kidding me?" She looked around to be sure her shocked exclamation hadn't piqued anyone's interest.

"Nope. And some of her"—he made air quotes with his fingers—"withdrawals match the same amounts as monthly cash deposits into Gladys's account."

That made so much more sense than thinking Irene was making blackmail payments to cover up the fact that Carter was living on development land and Ben was running a business from his home. Even if she was complicit by looking the other way. "Can you tell how long she's been stealing?"

"Since long before what I suspect were payments to Gladys began."

So, that's what Gladys had on her. She must have found out Irene was siphoning money from the HOA fees and called her out on it. Gia could see where Irene would have paid Gladys to keep quiet, considering she'd not only lose her job but likely end up in prison, which, if her conversation with Scott was any indication, she knew. "Do you think Scott Hoffmeier was involved?"

Alfie seemed to contemplate for a moment. "I mean, not that I can find. He did make regular monthly payments to Gladys, but that could also have simply been spousal support after the divorce. As far as linking him to Gladys or the HOA, I can't find any connection. Yet."

Still, if he was involved, it was definitely something that could get him disbarred. Gia wrestled with what to do with the information. She didn't want to see Alfie get in trouble, which he most definitely would if anyone found out he was hacking business records and personal bank accounts, but at the same time, there was no way Gia could leave Savannah to look into anything herself. Which, considering the attack in the parking lot, might well be for the best. "I want you to keep this to yourself, okay? Promise me you won't say anything to anyone."

"Gia, I—"

"I'm sorry, Alfie, but we have to let Hunt know. I'm going to tell him I found the information." Not that she wanted to lie to him, but she also couldn't jeopardize his career by putting him in the position of having to make a decision about what to do with Alfie, nor could she allow Alfie to risk going to prison.

"Gia . . ." When she started to stand, to step outside and make the call where no one in the packed waiting room would overhear, Alfie gripped her wrist. "Hey, I already emailed him the information and texted him to let him know."

"Alfie . . ." Her breathing hitched. "Won't you get in trouble?"

He shrugged, his jaw clenched defiantly. "Someone shot Leo and attacked you."

She slumped back into the seat and turned her hand over to weave her fingers with his. All she could manage was a harshly whispered, "Thank you, Alfie."

He gently closed the laptop cover then gripped her arm with his free hand and tilted his head against her shoulder. Then, he simply sat quietly with her and waited.

When Gia glanced toward the doorway for the millionth time to see if the doctor was coming, she spotted Donna Mae just walking in. And beside her, gripping her hand like a lifeline, stood Harley. Gia nudged Savannah's arm. "Savannah, look."

Savannah lifted her head. The instant she spotted Harley, she was on her feet. She bolted across the room with Gia right on her heels and flung herself into Harley's arms. "Oh, Harley, thank you so much for coming. I can't believe you did, but thank you."

He closed his eyes, hugged her close, and rested his chin on her shoulder. He said nothing, simply held her while she sobbed against his chest.

Donna Mae kept a hand on his arm, a constant reassurance that she was there for him, and spoke quietly to Gia. "He insisted on coming. No matter how hard I tried to talk him out of it, no matter that I told him I'd go for him and let Savannah know he was thinking of her, no matter how anxious he got as we approached the entrance, he insisted on being here for her."

Gia caught her trembling lower lip between her teeth and nodded.

Donna Mae wrapped her free arm around Gia's shoulders and tipped her head until it met Gia's. "He wanted me to tell you, the reason he doesn't like Carter is because Carter breaks the rules. He stays where he's not supposed to be. But he's never seen him hurt anyone, and he treats his dog really well, takes good care of him, even feeds him if he only has enough food for one."

That did not sound like a killer to Gia, someone who would put his pet's needs ahead of his own. So, what had he been doing fleeing the crime scene, not once but twice? What had he been looking for, and had someone put him up to it?

When Savannah stepped out of Harley's embrace, she swiped tears from her already raw cheeks with the heels of her hands. "Thank you so very much, Harley. I know how difficult it is for you to be inside, and I am so, so grateful. I will be sure to tell Leo you came for him, but now I want you to go with Donna Mae, okay? Let her take you outside where you'll be comfortable."

He nodded, sniffed, and wiped his tears. "I'll wait out front."

And Gia had no doubt he meant exactly that. He'd find a bench and sit in front of the hospital until he knew that Leo was out of surgery and going to make it and Savannah was okay. And, if he felt like she needed him, he'd come right back in to her.

Savannah reached up, slid a few strands of his mostly gray hair out of his face, and smiled warmly. "I'll make sure someone comes to tell you right away, as soon as we hear from the doctor."

He covered her hand with his own against his cheek, leaned into her touch for a moment, then turned away and limped down the corridor with Donna Mae's hand clutched in an iron grip.

Gia watched until they turned through the door into the stairwell. "You okay?"

Savannah sucked in a deep shaky breath and blew it out slowly. "I am. Yes. Thank you."

"You've helped him, you know."

"Not as much as he's helped me."

"Harley saved your life, and mine, but I think having people to care about and who care about him after so many years has helped him."

"I hope you're right." She turned away from the stairwell he'd disappeared into then froze, her expression tortured.

Gia looked over her shoulder to see what had her so upset.

A doctor strode toward them, her expression neutral, her dark hair pulled into a severe bun.

Gia held her breath. *Oh, God, please let Leo have made it through the surgery.*

When the doctor reached them, she scanned the crowded hallway, the packed waiting room. "Mrs. Dupont."

Savannah nodded.

Most people had stood. Every last set of eyes clung to the doctor. And no one uttered a single sound. Anticipation hung in the air, the weight almost crushing.

"I'm Dr. Bernard." She lay a hand on Savannah's upper arm. "Would you come with me, please?"

Savannah groped blindly behind her, and Gia slid a hand into hers. Together, they walked with the doctor down the hallway toward whatever fate waited.

Chapter Twenty-one

Gia sat on the cool tile floor with her legs folded and her back against the wall in the corridor outside the recovery room. The doctor had informed them the surgery had gone well, and had agreed to allow Savannah to stay with Leo in recovery, but Gia would have to wait outside. She'd assured Savannah that she'd update everyone else, then wait right outside the room until Savannah needed her.

As promised, she'd gone to the waiting room and updated everyone, telling them Leo had made it through the surgery and the doctor was optimistic he'd make a full recovery. Then, among the cheers and tears, Gia had broken down, completely overwhelmed with love and faith that everything would be okay, and that Leo would pull through. With that realization also came the certainty that she was exactly where she was meant to be, doing exactly what she was supposed to be doing. She'd experienced a sense of community and caring she'd never before known. And she would never give that up for anything in the world. Then she'd gone outside to update Harley and Donna Mae.

Gia inhaled deeply, still reeling from the roller coaster of emotions she'd been through over the past couple of days. She tilted her head back against the wall, closed her eyes, and breathed in the scent of disinfectant as she listened to the somehow muted hustle and bustle. Nurses' soft soles whispered against the tile floor, life-support equipment hummed and beeped, and voices carried in hushed tones.

When she stretched her legs out in front of her, every muscle in her body screamed in protest. The adrenaline coursing through her while they'd awaited word about Leo had dissipated, leaving her exhausted and beat up. She wanted nothing more than a hot bath and a good night's sleep. But neither of those things would happen until Gladys's killer, Leo's shooter, and Gia's attacker had been caught and put behind bars where they couldn't hurt anyone else.

At the sound of footsteps, she opened her eyes to find Hunt striding down the corridor. Had he found whoever had done this? Was he coming to tell her he'd made an arrest? Even as the questions flickered through her mind, she dismissed them. All that mattered in that moment was being in his arms. Ignoring the protests from her aching body, she climbed gingerly to her feet.

The instant he reached her, he opened his arms and pulled her into his embrace. He held her tightly yet gently, cocooning her in safety and love. Any semblance of control she'd clung to so fiercely fled as she collapsed against his chest and sobbed.

"Shh . . . It's all right, Gia." He smoothed her hair, kissed her head. "Everything's going to be okay. Are you all right?"

She nodded against him.

He held her another moment then set her back, gripping both her upper arms as he examined her from head to toe. "You're sure you're okay?"

"I am, Hunt. Tired, sore, and a little emotional." She half laughed through the tears. "But I'm fine. And Leo's going to be okay too."

"I know. I've been in touch with the hospital for regular updates." He stepped back, raked a hand through hair that stuck up in tufts. "I'm sorry I couldn't get here sooner, Gia. You do know I'd have been here for you if I could have, right?"

"Of course I do." And it almost surprised her how absolutely certain she was about that. There had been a time, not that long ago, when she'd thought she would never trust anyone again. "I'm really okay, Hunt. And while I had to be here for Savannah, it was more important for you to be out there searching for whoever did this."

"You know, Gia, I don't know what I'd have done tonight if I didn't know you were here with my cousin. She means the world to me, and it would have been so much more difficult for me to do what I had to do tonight if I didn't know you were here to take care of her. So, thank you."

"You don't ever have to thank me for that, Hunt. Savannah is my best friend in the world, she's family, and there's nothing I wouldn't do for her. Or you."

He held her gaze, searching for something so deep in her eyes she'd swear he could see to her very soul. "I love you, Gia. With all of my heart."

"I love you too, Hunt, with everything in me."

"I don't want to wait to marry you. If you have your heart set on a big wedding, surrounded by family and friends, I'll wait until you can set that up. If not, I'd go to the chapel right now and take our vows."

Her heart skipped, fluttered, then settled. "As much as I would love that, Hunt . . ."

His smile widened, touched his eyes with a hint of mischief. "Savannah would kill us."

Gia couldn't help but laugh. "While that is absolutely true, I could live with it. But I couldn't live with the fact that it would hurt her."

"No, me neither."

"So . . ." She weaved her fingers into his thick hair, pulled him close, and kissed him. When she finally pulled away, she smiled, and her heart felt lighter than it had in as long as she could remember. "You'll be happy to know I already gave the go-ahead."

"You . . ." He went completely still. "Seriously?"

"Yup." She gazed deep into his eyes, willing him to understand how much she loved him despite her hesitation. "I can't wait to be Mrs. Hunter Quinn. And I told Savannah and Trevor to set something up as soon as possible. I was waiting for the perfect opportunity to tell you, maybe over a nice romantic dinner, but with everything that's been happening lately, there just hasn't been a free moment."

His smile spread slowly and he pulled her close, kissed her head, then set her back, held her arms and studied her as if she might change her mind and bolt at any moment.

But she'd never been more sure of anything.

"None of that matters. I'm just thrilled you're finally ready to stop dragging your feet."

"I'm sorry it took so long, Hunt. I can't even say for sure why it did. I have no doubts about my feelings for you."

"I know that." He smoothed her hair, cradled her cheek, seemed to need the contact. "But you were afraid. Understandably so after what you've been through."

"Thank you so much for understanding and for being patient."

"Always." He kissed her, just a gentle peck on the cheek but filled with emotion, then cleared his throat. "So, you think Savannah will be okay with a small shotgun wedding, even though she won't get to spend months planning something extravagant and amazing?"

Savannah's words from earlier came back to her, along with a moment of absolute panic, but then she settled. Surely, Savannah would understand if she wanted to wait a little longer to have kids. Probably. She hoped. Well, that was a problem for another day. She didn't have to tell Savannah her plans just yet. "I'm pretty sure she'll be just fine. Can you stay a few minutes?"

"Yes. But why don't you sit. You look beat."

"Thanks." She grinned, but he looked pretty beat up himself, and there was no telling how long either of them would have to keep going. With that in mind, she slid down the wall to sit shoulder to shoulder with Hunt, his legs stretched out in front of him, one ankle crossed over the other. Just having him there at her side, her rock, brought her the strength she'd need to get through whatever would come next. She rested her head against his shoulder.

"Did you find whoever shot Leo?" Though she already knew the answer. He'd have told her right away if he had, even if only by text.

"I can't be sure, but I think so."

She lurched upright and spun to face him. "You did? Why didn't you call or text me?"

He sighed, obviously realizing their moment of peace had come to an end. "I needed to see you, needed to know for myself that you were okay. And I wanted to come tell you in person. Plus, I needed to come check on Savannah. She's holding up okay?"

"Her strength sometimes amazes me."

"Yeah, me too."

She almost slipped, wanted so badly to reveal the news that Savannah was going to be a mother, wanted him to know his cousin was even stronger than he realized. But that wasn't her news to share. "She's doing okay, Hunt. And, when it's all over and Leo is home and on the road to recovery, she's going to be fine."

He nodded, swallowed hard. "Okay. Anyway, Alfie was really the one who gave us our break."

"He's not going to be in trouble, is he?"

"Nope. I've seen to it he'll be okay, and he won't be punished for any information he accessed and provided."

"How'd you manage that?" Because he'd broken any number of laws.

Hunt grinned. "I hired him."

A laugh blurted out before she could stop it. "You did what?"

"I hired him as a consultant. For this case, I'm going to use him as an anonymous source, but moving forward, that boy is too talented not to have on our side." He sobered quickly. "The information he provided allowed us to bring everyone in for questioning. And, while we would have eventually been able to access the sources he did, my techs were held up waiting for warrants. For now, though, we do have your attackers in custody."

"You do?"

He nodded. "Between the information from Alfie and the picture Cybil was able to get of the van leaving the parking lot, which we were able to trace to the Rolling Pines Homeowners Association, we were able to pick Irene up for questioning."

Although it saddened her, Gia wasn't really surprised. The woman had a lot at stake.

"And she threw her companion, Scott Hoffmeier, under the bus before we even got her into the interrogation room."

Thinking back to the argument she'd overheard, that wasn't really surprising either. "Do you know which one of them killed Gladys and shot Leo?"

Hunt scowled. "That's the thing. Irene and Scott both confessed to the attack on you, but neither of them owned up to shooting Leo or killing Gladys. Neither of them was sorry to see her go, and they were both real quick to admit to being relieved when they'd heard the news, but they both vehemently deny any involvement."

"And you believe them?"

"I honestly don't know." He lifted his hands, shrugged, then lowered them. "While I'd love to think I have the killer in custody, I just can't be a hundred percent sure. At least, not yet."

"Well, if they didn't kill Gladys or shoot Leo, why did they attack me?" She frowned, trying to think back to what seemed like ages ago but had actually only been about twelve hours. "They were looking for something."

"Apparently, according to them, Gladys kept a spreadsheet in a black notebook. She had no digital record, only the physical copy, and it contained a list of names, infractions, and payments for everyone she was blackmailing. They were terrified the police would find it and discover all of their indiscretions. With Gladys gone, they figured if they could get their hands on the book, they'd be in the clear."

"So, what made them think I'd know where to find it? I didn't even find out about the blackmail until after Gladys had been killed." Though she suspected she'd have learned about it soon enough if she hadn't been killed.

"Apparently, Carter was walking his dog the morning Gladys went over to your house. As soon as he saw her marching across the street, he bolted into the woods, afraid of another run-in with her."

"Have you spoken to him?"

He nodded. "I questioned him myself. He says he saw her carrying the book when she was headed to your house. He lingered on the edge of the forest to see what she was doing, if she was going to blackmail you too, but he wasn't looking at her the whole time, he was keeping an eye on Ben, who was also watching the drama unfold."

"And he didn't see what she did with the book?" Yet another disappointment. But at least they had something now.

"Nope. Just that she didn't have it when she went back home." He looked her in the eye. "Gia, look, is there any chance Gladys knew someone was after her? Could she have left the book somewhere in your house for safekeeping?"

She tried to think back to that morning. It seemed so far distant, and so much had happened since, she couldn't even bring the interaction into focus. "Not that I know of. She didn't even come in the house. That, I do know, because I never would have let her in with Thor."

"And you didn't find anything anywhere on the porch or around the house anywhere when you and Alfie were installing the cameras?"

"No. Nothing. If we had, I would have turned it over to you right away." Well, except for the notepad. In her defense, though, she had turned in the pearl earring.

He sat back, wrapped an arm around her, and pulled her close. "I do know that, Gia. I hope you understand I still had to ask."

"Of course." Gia nestled against him, comforted by his presence and the fact that all of this might almost be behind them. "If you want, you can search around my house, or even go in, but I know she couldn't have gotten anything inside."

"Thanks, Gia. I appreciate that. I am going to have to look, and it will go much faster if I have your permission and don't have to wait for a warrant."

"No problem. Believe me, I want this over. I want you to find whoever killed Gladys and hurt Leo and send them to prison for what they did." She wanted to see whoever it was pay for the pain they'd caused Savannah at what should have been one of the happiest moments of her life.

"And we will. But, in the meantime . . ." He smoothed a hand over her hair, kissed her temple. "I still want you to be careful. Until we know if we have the killer in custody, there could still be someone out there willing to kill to cover up a secret."

The thought dashed ice cold on her warm and fuzzies. She shivered at the thought that a killer could still not only be on the loose and searching for Gladys's book, but think whatever secrets it held might somehow be in Gia's possession. "I'll be careful. But do you think there's a chance Carter is mistaken?"

"Anything's possible. He could be mistaken, he could be lying . . ." He shrugged, distracted as he shot off a text, then he looked past her, stood, and pulled her to her feet.

"Could he have killed her?"

"It's possible. He has no alibi, but I had no reason to hold him, so I had to let him go."

A nurse hurried down the hallway, then stopped when she reached them and smiled. "You must be Gia."

She nodded.

"Savannah asked me to come let you know they just transferred Leo to a room. He's recovering nicely, and she went with him, but she'd like you to meet her there."

Her breath whooshed out in a rush of relief. She and Hunt thanked her and followed her directions to the second floor. When they arrived at Leo's door, Gia knocked on the doorjamb and poked her head inside. "Hey. Is this a bad time?"

Leo sat up in bed, Savannah in a chair beside him clutching his hand. She smiled when she spotted Gia and Hunt. "Actually, it's the perfect time. Come on in, please. You're just in time."

"Just in time for what?"

"Shut the door behind you."

Gia did as she asked, then approached the bed. "How do you feel, Leo?"

"Like I got shot." He grinned. "I'm okay, though."

"I'm so glad." She hugged him, carful not to hurt him.

Hunt did the same, then stood with her at the side of the bed.

Savannah shifted to sit on the bed beside Leo. She held one of his hands in both of hers. "What I am about to say does not leave this room. You are all sworn to secrecy until I'm ready. Okay?"

Hunt frowned at Gia, but she simply shook her head as joy swelled through her.

"Leo, I'm so sorry to spring this on you right now, and maybe I'm being selfish, and if I am, I'm sorry, but I should have told you right away, and I didn't, and I'm sorry for that too. It's just, I wanted to have a special moment . . ." She sniffed, lowered her gaze. Her tears dripped onto their clasped hands.

Gia lay a hand on her shoulder. "Do you want Hunt and me to go?"

Savannah reached up and grabbed her hand. "No. Please, stay."

"Okay." She stepped back to give Savannah space.

She summoned her strength and smiled at Leo. "You need to get better as quickly as possible and get home to me."

"You know I will."

"You have to get home to us."

He frowned.

"You're going to be a daddy." She sobbed. "The best daddy in the world."

Leo's breathing hitched, sending the heart monitor beeping, and he half laughed, half groaned as Savannah flung herself into his arms.

She lifted her head for just a moment to look at him. "Does this mean you're happy?"

"My love, I have never been happier."

Chapter Twenty-two

As she unlocked her front door, Gia's eyes burned, though whether from a residual effect of the bear spray or total exhaustion, she had no idea. Still, she couldn't help but smile every time she thought of Savannah and Leo and the joy they shared. At the moment, though, the thought of snuggling in her warm, comfy bed nearly had her weeping. But she couldn't rest yet. She'd promised Hunt she'd get what she needed for a night at the hospital with Savannah, stop by Trevor's to check on Thor, Klondike, and Pepper, then get back to the hospital. Even though Hunt had already let her know his men had searched the property and not found Gladys's blackmail book, she still glanced around the front patio where Gladys had stood.

She shoved the front door open, then turned and stood in the doorway the same way she had when Gladys had visited. She remembered keeping the door nearly shut because she didn't want to risk Thor getting out. She eased it shut a bit. She'd mostly stared directly at Gladys's face, shocked by her threats. But then she'd shoved her back. Or poked her, really. Had Gladys been holding anything at the time? She tried to envision the scene. No matter how she tried, she couldn't recall Gladys holding anything.

Carter Marx must have either made a mistake or lied. But did lying to the police make him a killer? She scanned the area for any sign he was watching, but she saw no one. The development was quiet. She averted her gaze when it fell on the mess still at Miley's and wondered if Miley would stay after all that had gone on. She had to admit, if it were her, she'd probably move out. A pang of regret hit her that she hadn't taken the time to get to know the woman who lived right across the street from her better. With a sigh, she turned her attention away from Miley's house and closer to her own.

Despite the fact that the police had already done so, she conducted a cursory search. She looked behind and under the bushes against the front of the house, even lifted the lid of the hose holder—nothing. And there simply weren't that many places to search. So, unless Rocky had made off with it, Gladys must have hidden the book somewhere else.

Giving up the search, she walked inside and swung the door shut behind her.

Since Savannah planned to spend the night at the hospital with Leo, Gia had offered to run to her house and pack a few things for them, but she needed a couple minutes for herself as well. She'd forgo a shower for the sake of expediency, but she refused to wear the clothes she'd rolled around the parking lot in for another minute. Although Trevor had offered her a room at his house with Thor and the cats, she'd politely thanked him but declined—for tonight, at least. She'd spend one more night at the hospital, probably curled up on a waiting room couch somewhere so she'd be close by if Leo took a turn for the worse or Savannah needed her.

With that in mind, she changed into comfy sweats and an oversized T-shirt and brushed her teeth. She rummaged through her closet for a duffle bag, then set it on the bed. She tossed in a pair of fluffy socks, a throw pillow from her bed, and her e-reader. Maybe she'd actually get to finish a novel for once. She started to close the bag, then grabbed a throw from the back of a chair and stuffed that in as well. She'd never understand why they kept hospitals so cold, but she had no intention of spending another night with her teeth chattering. She took one last look around to be sure there was nothing else she'd need. Satisfied she could make do with what she had, she zipped up the duffle bag and set it beside the door.

A quick circuit through the kitchen and living room assured here Zoe and Trevor had taken everything Thor and Klondike could need.

A knock at the front door startled her, and she jumped, pressed a hand against her chest to keep her heart from leaping out, and wondered how long it would be before a knock on the door brought pleasure rather than panic. Then again, there was still the possibility a killer lurked in Rolling Pines.

She parted the curtain and peered out the window.

Ben Stettler stood on the front patio, hands on his hips, back to the door as he studied the house across the street. She'd promised Hunt she'd be careful, but surely he'd eliminated Ben as a suspect. The man had saved Leo's life. If not for him . . .

She shivered and swung the front door open but stopped short of inviting him in. Although some guilt tried to surface, she shoved it back down. Until they knew for sure who'd killed Gladys and shot

Leo, she couldn't fully trust anyone. "Hey, Ben. How are you doing?"

"I'm fine, but I'm concerned about you. How are you holding up?"

"I'm doing okay, actually. I just came from the hospital, and Leo is doing well."

"Oh, that is wonderful news. I'm so glad to hear it. And Savannah? How is she holding up?"

"About as well as can be expected. She's tired, but I think she'll sleep well tonight now that Leo is out of immediate danger." She paused, the scene from last night playing through her mind as she looked past him to the spot where Leo had gone down. "Ben, I know Savannah and I have both already thanked you, but thank you again. It's terrifying to think what might have happened if you weren't there."

"It's no problem. I'm just glad I was there and had the knowledge to help." He shoved his hands into his overall pockets and rocked back on his heels.

"Anyway, I don't mean to be rude, but I'm just on my way out. I have to get back to the hospital."

"No problem at all. I really just wanted to check in. And, please, if you need anything, don't hesitate to call." He held out a hand, which Gia took, then gave her a quick one-armed hug.

"Thank you."

She stood by the door for a moment, watching him go. When this was all said and done, she was going to make an effort to get to know her neighbors, the people who'd all come out to help when there had been trouble. As Ben crossed his yard, he spared a long glance in the direction where Leo had been shot, shook his head, then continued into his house.

She shut the door and made a quick round of the house to be sure all of the doors and windows were locked. She'd do the same at Savannah's when she stopped for her things, just to be on the safe side. Though it saddened her that it might be a while before either of them would feel safe in their own homes. Since she'd left her purse in the car, and couldn't think of anything else she needed, she hefted the duffle bag over her shoulder.

Another knock sounded at the door. Thinking Ben had returned, she opened it and smiled. Her smile faltered, but only for a moment, when she found Miley standing there. "Oh, hey, Miley."

"Hi, Gia. Umm . . ." She glanced back over her shoulder toward her own house, and Gia felt a pang of pity. Whether from her sister's death or the pending investigation or her coming divorce, or even some combination of all three, Miley looked haggard. Her eyes sank into dark circles, her hair hung in limp strands, and deep lines bracketed her mouth.

"Is everything okay, Miley?"

"No. No, Gia, it's really not." She smoothed a shaking hand over her hair. "Can I come in for a minute?"

Gia started to step back and invite her inside, but alarm bells clanged in her head. She'd promised Hunt she'd be careful, and there was still possibly a killer on the loose. She reminded herself that Miley had motive to have killed her sister, maybe more than most. She'd taken Gladys in, supported her for six months, and Gladys had repaid her by cheating with Miley's husband and blackmailing all of her neighbors. But would that be enough to justify murder in her mind? Based on the woman she'd sort of known, and the woman she'd met in the café, she'd have said no. But this bedraggled, desperate-looking woman—maybe.

"I'm sorry, Miley. I'm just on my way back to the hospital, and I'm in a hurry." Gia started to step outside, to pull the door shut behind her.

Miley blocked her path. "I'm sorry, Gia, but I'm afraid I'm going to have to insist."

"You—?"

Miley pulled a handgun from her pocket, keeping it close in front of her so even if someone did happen to pass by in that moment, they wouldn't see anything or realize anything was amiss.

"Miley, I—"

"Now, Gia." She poked her rib with the gun, and Gia stumbled back into the foyer with Miley moving in tandem. "Please, don't make me shoot you."

Gia realized her mistake as soon as Miley closed the door behind her. She should have taken a stand and fought on the patio, hoped someone would notice, because now she was at a killer's mercy. And there was no way she'd let her live. Gia could identify her.

"I know what you're thinking, and I'm not going to kill you if you just do as I ask. I will tie you up and walk out of here. By the time you manage to free yourself or someone realizes you're missing and comes looking for you, I'll be long gone."

"Okay, what is it you want?"

"Gladys's book."

"Then I'm afraid we have a problem, because I don't have the book, nor have I ever seen it."

"I know she brought it over here, Gia. I saw her leave the house with it that morning, and she didn't go anywhere else but straight here and then back home. I tried searching when you weren't home, but I couldn't find it anywhere outside, so it must be in here. It has to be," she muttered to herself, looking around the small foyer.

"Miley, listen, why don't we go in the kitchen, have a cup of tea, and talk about this. You can tell me—"

"I'll tell you nothing!" Spittle sprayed from her mouth. "I know it's here. She was good at hiding things, my sister, always squirreling away tidbits in her little hidey-holes. Then she'd use them against me, always trying to get me into trouble with our dad. All because she was jealous that he'd left her and her mother and married my mom, stayed to raise me. She blamed me. As if my father's choices were my fault. She hated me for that. But did that stop her from showing up on my doorstep when she was desperate for help?"

Gia needed to calm her down, to somehow deescalate the situation before she accidentally fired the weapon she so casually waved around with her finger on the trigger. "I can see where that would be upsetting for you."

"Upsetting? Are you kidding me? That woman ruined my life, and even after she moved in with me and made a nuisance of herself with half the neighborhood, made me a laughingstock among all of my friends, and cheated with my husband, it still wasn't enough for her."

"What do you mean?" Gia had to keep her talking. Sooner or later, Savannah would realize she was taking too long and let Hunt know. He'd come looking for her, of that she had no doubt, if she could just keep Miley occupied long enough.

"Even after all of that, she went through my belongings when I wasn't home, found love letters from an old boyfriend that I'd forgotten all about, and threatened to give them to Elijah to use against me in our divorce. The letters weren't dated, so I couldn't prove they weren't recent. And then, she calmly opened her book on my kitchen table, added my name to her spreadsheet, and told me how much she expected me to pay her each month while she continued to freeload off me." She shook her head, pressed the heel of her gun hand against her temple with the barrel pointed up toward the ceiling.

Gia contemplated rushing her, but she couldn't risk it. Miley was clearly not in her right mind, and she might well shoot Gia if she startled her. "I'll tell you what. Why don't we search the house? Honestly, I didn't see her with a book that day, but she had me so upset, I'll admit I might not have noticed it. The police already searched outside, and so did I, but no one has searched inside. Why don't we do it together?"

She frowned, lowered her hand to her side, gun pointing toward the floor.

Gia gauged the distance.

"You'd help me?"

"Of course. You've already been through so much. I don't want to see you hurt any more than you already have been." And it surprised her to realize that was true. Not that she'd ever condone murder, but she couldn't help feeling sorry for Miley. Clearly, Gladys had pushed her past her breaking point. Still, there were a hundred other ways she could have handled the situation. She could have thrown her out, gone to the police with evidence she was blackmailing people . . . anything but kill her.

"And just so you know . . ." Her breath hitched. "I didn't shoot Leo on purpose."

Any ounce of sympathy shriveled and died. "You shot Leo?"

"I didn't mean it. I told you, it was an accident. After I'm gone, you have to tell Savannah and Leo both how sorry I am. I panicked, thought he'd come to arrest me." A sob tore free, and she squeezed her eyes closed.

Gia pounced, grabbed her wrist in both hands, and tried to wrestle the gun free.

Her front window imploded, glass spraying everywhere.

Miley whirled toward the sound and lost her grip on the weapon. The gun clattered to the floor.

"Freeze! Don't move, Miley!" Hunt stood in the window with his weapon aimed at Miley's chest.

She continued to cry and mutter to herself.

Ben climbed through the front window and opened the door to Hunt.

As he moved into the doorway, gun still drawn, Miley lurched toward him.

Gia swung with all her might, and her fist connected hard with Miley's jaw.

The woman's head snapped back, and she dropped like a rock.

Gia looked up at Hunt. Thoughts tumbled through her mind too fast to process, emotions threatening to overwhelm her: the fear she'd felt upon hearing Ben's call go out over the police scanner, the horror at finding Leo lying so still on the ground, the pain that had so filled Savannah when she'd told Gia she was pregnant and knew she might never get to share that joy with her husband. For just one moment, she wished Miley would get back up so she could hit her again.

And then Hunt was beside her.

"Give me the cuffs, Hunt. I've got this." Ben took the handcuffs Hunt offered, then crouched beside Miley, rolled her over, and cuffed her hands behind her back before she regained consciousness.

Gia looked Hunt in the eye, her voice quivering. "That was for Savannah."

Chapter Twenty-Three

Although the café was closed, laughter and joy filled the dining room. Leo had been released from the hospital, and he and Savannah sat at the big round table Gia considered her family table, surrounded by friends and loved ones.

Cole laughed out loud, a deep, contagious belly laugh that had Gia smiling.

Gia stood behind the counter, loading plates and glasses onto a tray to bring to the table. Even though she and Cole had both offered to cook, Hunt had insisted he'd bring takeout instead, give them all a chance to relax and enjoy themselves.

"Hey! Food's here!" Cole stood and went to unlock the door for Hunt.

Gia set the tray down and turned to find Hunt walking in with a stack of pizza boxes. "Seriously? Pizza?"

He frowned at the boxes. "What's wrong with pizza? Besides, that's what Leo wanted, so that's what he gets."

Since she couldn't argue that, she simply shook her head and took the top few boxes from him. "Come on, we'll set them up along the counter buffet-style, and everyone can grab what they want and go sit."

He kissed her cheek. "Sounds good to me."

She set the stack of boxes on one side of the counter and went to move the covered pastry dishes out of the way to make room. "Any news?"

"Yeah." Despite the fact that they were among friends, Hunt slid onto a stool and spoke quietly. "The DNA results from Ben's hammer came back."

Her heart skipped. "And?"

"And it was the weapon used to kill Gladys."

Everything in her went perfectly still as she stared at him. "You can't possibly think Ben killed her. Miley all but confessed to murdering her."

He held his hands up. "Yes, she did. She signed a full confession and admitted everything that went on that night."

She let out a sigh of relief. She'd come to like Ben, who currently sat at a place of honor next to Leo. Plus, he'd not only saved Leo's life but Gia's as well. If he hadn't seen Miley force Gia into her house and called Hunt, things might have ended much differently.

"Miley came upon Gladys out back that night, looking at the holes that Thor had supposedly dug. They argued more about the love letters, and Gladys told Miley she could get out if she didn't like the arrangement."

Gia's eyes went wide. "She threw her out of her own house?"

"Apparently."

"What did Miley do?"

"She stormed away, across Ben's lawn, and saw his garage door open with the lights on. Apparently, he sometimes forgets to shut the door if he's working in one of the back sheds and goes in the back door."

Which explained why the garage had been standing open the night Gia had gone over.

"Miley went inside, grabbed the hammer from the tool bench, and went back to hide in the hedges to attack Gladys."

He didn't have to say any more. Gia already knew the rest. And it was a sad story, but still . . . . She could have turned herself in afterward, could have told the police what happened. Instead, when she'd felt backed into a corner, she'd shot Leo. Her gaze skipped to where he sat with Savannah close at his side, where she'd been ever since he'd been shot. Gia had no doubt she'd come back to work eventually, but for now she was exactly where she needed to be.

"Afterward, she wiped the hammer down in the grass and returned it to Ben's garage." He shrugged. "Either she didn't think anyone would notice, or she thought we'd figure it was his and he'd killed Gladys."

Unbelievable. And to think, she'd felt sorry for Miley. But the woman had no care for anyone other than herself, didn't care who ended up being collateral damage.

When people began filling their plates, Hunt gestured for her to move away. She shifted down toward the register. "Something else?"

"Yeah." Hunt wrapped a finger in a few strands of her hair and tugged gently. "We have Gladys's blackmail book."

"You found it?"

"Carter Marx brought it in. Apparently, he saw her bring it to your house that morning, in an effort to blackmail you. At least, according to Miley . . ."

Oh, right. She'd forgotten to tell Hunt about her suspicions. Thankfully, he let it drop without asking what she'd have done, since she still had no answer.

"Carter saw her hide the book in the bushes in front of your house. No one knows why, maybe because she was afraid Miley would find it, but he went and retrieved it when you left."

"Why?"

"He thought he could stop the blackmail if he took the book. Then, after Gladys was killed, he figured that was the end of it, and no one needed to see whatever secrets she'd written there. He didn't want to see anyone get into trouble. Then, when Leo was shot, he was afraid to come forward, afraid we'd think he had something to do with the shooting."

Gia felt bad for him. It seemed he'd tried to do the right thing.

"But after Miley was arrested, he brought the book into the station and explained to me what had happened." He smiled and tucked the hair behind her ear, then leaned his elbows on the counter. "And he asked me to tell you he's sorry. He thinks it was his fault Gladys gave you a hard time, because he'd been digging up her yard searching for the book."

"Is he going to be charged with anything?"

"Not unless you want to press charges, since technically he came onto your property and took the book."

She waved that off. Honestly, she just wanted to put this whole thing behind her and move on. "Will Scott and Irene be prosecuted for attacking me?"

He firmed his lips into a thin line. "Yes. Absolutely. That's non-negotiable."

She figured it best not to argue the point. She'd been terrified when they'd attacked her in the parking lot, and they should pay for that.

"And Irene has been charged with theft as well, for misappropriating the funds from the HOA."

"I know what Gladys had on Irene, but did you find out what she was holding over Scott's head?"

"He cheated on the bar exam and would absolutely have been

disbarred if she'd come forward with the information."

"Will Miley be charged with first-degree murder?"

"Probably second degree, since we can't really prove premeditation and intent. But she'll also be charged with the attempted murder of a police officer, so she's going away for a long time regardless."

Gia could live with that. In the meantime . . .

Trevor and Zoe approached, and it was time to forget about murder and enjoy her friends. "What's up, guys? Did you get pizza?"

"We were about to, but there's something we wanted to tell you first." Trevor lifted their clasped hands, kissed Zoe's knuckles.

"What's up?"

"Savannah told us you want us to plan your wedding for as soon as possible, and that's no problem." Trevor grinned, making puppy eyes at Zoe.

She released his hand, wiggled her fingers, and squealed.

Gia joined her when she noted the diamond on her left ring finger, then hugged them both. "Oh, I am so happy for you both. Congratulations!"

"Yeah, congratulations, guys. That's great." Hunt shook Trevor's hand, hugged Zoe.

"Does everyone know already?"

"Pretty much, but we wanted to get to tell you ourselves before you opened the café tomorrow and the Bailey sisters could beat us to it." Trevor laughed.

"Well, thank you for that. And I couldn't be happier."

"We're going to plan our wedding right after yours."

"Well, there's more good news happening somewhere in there too, so that pizza's going to have to hold on for a minute. Come on." Gia led the small group to the table where everyone was gathered, grabbed a glass and a fork from the tray, held up the glass and tapped it lightly. "Can I have your attention."

The room quieted, and she nodded toward Savannah.

Savannah hooked her arm through Leo's as they stood. "I asked Gia to bring everyone together tonight, because all of you stood by us during what could have been an awful tragedy, and I can't tell you how much that meant to us. When Leo was shot, my world came screaming to a halt. And because all of you pitched in, offered support, sent meals, and cared for us, I was able to spend every minute with Leo. So, I just want to say thank you and to ask you all to stand with us again, this time in a joyous occasion, when we welcome our child into this amazing community."

About the Author

Lena Gregory is the author of the Bay Island Psychic Mystery series, which takes place on a small island between the north and south forks of Long Island, New York, and the All-Day Breakfast Café Mystery series, which is set on the outskirts of Florida's Ocala National Forest.

Lena Grew up in a small town on the south shore of eastern Long Island, where she still lives with her husband, three kids, son-in-law, and five dogs, and works full-time as a writer and freelance editor.

To learn more about Lena and her latest writing endeavors, visit her website at www.lenagregory.com/, and be sure to sign up for her newsletter at lenagregory.us12.list-manage.com/subscribe?u=9765d0711ed4fab4fa31b16ac&id=49d42335d1.